Trimble

MW01681148

...Forever and ever, AMEN

by Eleanor Grindstaff

Randall House Publications
P.O. Box 17306 • Nashville, TN 37217

...Forever and ever, AMEN

Randall House Publications
Nashville, Tennessee
ISBN 0-89265-136-9

Printed in the United States of America.

Dedication

I dedicate this book to two Free Will Baptists from Greene County, Tennessee, who mean a lot to me.

TRULA GUNTER CRONK
TERRY CLAY BAILEY

Foreword

When we read of pioneers, they are usually in covered wagons going across the Great Plains. They have adventures with the Indians. They struggle and have victories. If religion plays into the story, most of the time it deals with Calvinism.

But there were other pioneers. No state is as rich in pioneer heritage as Tennessee. The first settlers who came in didn't ride covered wagons. They walked, leading their animals up and down the mountainous terrain of the Southern Appalachians. They moved into the lower mountains and valleys of what is now East Tennessee. This group was also basically Scotch-Irish and Presbyterian. However, before Tennessee became a state in 1796, many Baptists had already moved into the area governed by the Watauga Assembly, as their newly formed democratic government was called. There is strong evidence that among these Baptists were those known as Freewillers.

My story is about a young boy caught up in the struggle of his times. His desire to be free and to get answers for his spiritual questions are the themes of this story. I have combined the rich history of Tennessee with the rich heritage of Free Will Baptists into a story for young people. The historical events are accurate. The organ and Indian episode did happen, although not in Tennessee, but in North Carolina. But, who knows? It could have happened here also.

I borrowed the name, "Guard," from a beloved uncle. I've always thought it was a very different and distinctive name. Matilda is an old family name. When I chose it, I had forgotten that Uncle Guard's wife, my Aunt Clara, was Clara Matilda. So I honor them both.

Chapter One

Guard's heart ached more than his back, and goodness knows that his back ached terribly. It seemed that he had never done anything but dig and cut weeds, up one row and down another...and all of this on a rocky hillside. He brushed away hot, salty tears, and looked about him. He was glad that no one was around to see him crying, or hear him talk to himself.

"Ma, why did you do this to me? Why did you sell me?"

But Guard knew why. After Pa had died, Ma just couldn't keep Guard and his brother, Garse. Ma had begun coughing a lot, just like Pa had done. Anyway, they had had to move from the tenement house, if you can call one room, a lean-to, and an attic, a house. It shook in the wind and was impossible to heat in the winter.

Memories of hard, yet good times, brought a torrent of tears. Their Pa and Ma loved them. Pa had laughed and played with them before he got sick. It seemed so long ago and so far away.

A garter snake slithered across Guard's bare feet. He awoke from his thoughts and suddenly became aware of his task. The lad knew that he had better get to work or else he would have to suffer the consequences. He began hoeing again. There seemed to be more rocks than dirt along here. And for every rock there was a weed. He wiped his sweaty face on his dirty, ragged shirt sleeve.

"Oh, Ma, I didn't mean to complain. I did so love you. I know that you loved me. You were so pretty, so bubbly with laughter and love. Ma, do you remember how I cried when that grand lady in town called us 'poor white trash'? You told me not to cry, that we were special, that God loved us. You said we had the things that money cannot buy. Ma, you told me that we loved each other.

"And Ma, I didn't cry when you died. I was brave, Ma. I didn't cry when they took Garse away. I haven't really cried in such a long time. I miss you, Ma, and I'm gonna try harder to get along with Mr. Forrester. Honest, I will. I only have two more years, and then I'll be free, Ma. I'm gonna find Garse. We're gonna be a family again."

Guard hoed weeds and pulled sage grass until he reached the end of the field. A few feet below the field a small branch tumbled from higher up a rocky incline. He put down his hoe and jumped down on the cool, damp moss. He lay on his stomach drinking from the cold water as the spray from the cascading water cooled his face, washing away his thoughts of self-pity. He felt the tired kinks relax in his shoulders. All the tiredness of the morning seemed to leave. He rolled over on his back on the cool moss and lay watching the clouds move swiftly through the shadowy silhouettes of the laurel bushes.

He was drifting off to sleep when a shadow fell over him, the moss, and the water. He opened his eyes expecting to be facing an angry Mr. Forrester. Instead, Guard was looking up into the face of a large man in buckskins, carrying a long, flintlock rifle. He jumped up, "Y-yes...sir...who...?"

"Howdy, Son, I'm looking for James Robertson. Does he live in these here parts? Now, don't answer yet, that water is just too invitin'. I need a long drink and a long rest. That there moss is just what I need fer a piller. What did ye say yer name is, Son?"

"I...I didn't say...but it's Guard McCall. Yes, sir, Mr. Robertson lives somewhere near here. I don't know zackly where. But I know hit's nearby, fer I hear 'em talking 'bout him."

The comfort of the moment was shattered with a loud, angry voice, "Guard, Ga-ard, you need a beatin', where you at? You lazy young'un. You needn't think you're gettin' by with all this here trifleness."

Guard hurried up the incline, "Yes, sir, Mr. Forrester, I's just getting a drink of water, 'fore I started 'nother row." He dodged as Mr. Forrester's hand swung at him.

A big arm swept from nowhere and caught Mr. Forrester's arm. "Now, jest slow down there," a forceful voice said slowly. "This here boy is givin' me aid. I'm alookin' fer James

Robertson and I just stopped here to get directions, and then I discovered this here cool water. That's fine, fine water fer a thirsty trail blazer. Now, I'll jest be on my way to town. Bye, now, Guard."

"Goodbye, Mr...?"

"Boone, Daniel Boone."

Daniel Boone slowly gathered up his backpack and his other bundles. Then he slowly and deliberately put them down again. He laid down on the moss for another long draught of water. It was as if he lingered to see what Mr. Forrester would do or say to Guard.

Mr. Forrester turned away, but not before he shook his fist in Guard's face. "Young man, you get that corn patch done, or your hide won't hold shucks. I'll see you back to the house come dark." He stormed through the rocks back to the cabin.

Guard could hear him cursing as he tromped across the field. He picked up his hoe and walked the few feet to the weedy patch of ground that was to be a corn patch. He half-heartedly struck at a clump of sage grass.

Mr. Boone watched him as he again gathered up his trail gear, "Be seein' you, Son," he said.

Guard wanted so badly to run after him and thank him. He wanted to ask him if all the things he had heard about the wilderness were true. He felt the embarrassment as it crept up over his face. But he got up the courage and called out, "Mr. Boone, wait, wait! Mr. Boone, is it true that there's land fer the askin' over the mountains?"

"Well, not zackly fer the askin'. It's more like land fer the workin'. Come down to the town square tonight and hear all about it."

Guard was surprised himself when he realized that he had the entire cornpatch hoed. Surely Mr. Forrester wouldn't be too upset. He would hurry in and get the stock fed and do the milking. If he tried, maybe, just maybe he could slip out and go hear Mr. Boone talk.

Mr. Forrester scowled and growled as Guard came into the yard. He muttered under his breath. "I knew that you'd be nuthin' but trouble when I took you in. Ye don't even earn your board and keep." He puckered his lips and aimed his tobacco juice for Guard's bare feet. Guard jumped, and Mr. Forrester missed.

Mr. Forrester laughed wickedly, "Yer learnin', but my aim

hain't so bad. Hit's a good thang that there big man was there or ye'd be sorry. Ye'd better of done a fair job of that corn patch or I'll give ye what fer. Now put that hoe up, get them chores done, grab yer grub, and get to bed. Hit's warm enough to get back in the hay loft. No use lettin' the likes of you clutter up the house when the barn'll do ye proud. Now, git!"

This was the break that Guard needed. He could slip out of the barn and not be missed. Only thing was, he'd have to try to keep from being seen in town. If anyone saw him, they'd be sure to mention it to Mr. Forrester, whether or not they meant him any harm.

As he worked he made mental plans. He finished the chores as quickly as possible and went to wash up in the rain barrel behind the barn. He bent over the barrel, and using his hands he dipped water over his dark auburn hair. His hair was stiff with dust and sweat. He washed it best as he could, shook it, and ran his fingers through it.

By now the water in the barrel had stilled enough to show his reflection. He wasn't bad looking. He was rather large for a boy almost seventeen years old. He was strong and muscular. Although his hair was dark auburn, his skin was well-tanned, not at all fair and sunburned like many who had red hair. His blue eyes had lost their laughter, and yet they had within them hidden hope and longing for better times.

He walked quickly toward the house. Mrs. Forrester gave him a tender look. Guard felt that she would have liked to be a friend, maybe even a mother to him. He felt that she was afraid of her husband. She smiled with her eyes as she handed him a dish of food. He took it, thanked her, and went into the barn.

The boy quickly ate and then nervously straightened up the barn. It seemed to him that Mr. Forrester would never go into his cabin. He waited until he went in and then just as he started to slip out he remembered that sometimes Mr. Forrester made a bedcheck on him. So he climbed the loft ladder and lay down in the hay.

Sure enough, in a few minutes, he heard Mr. Forrester enter the barn, and climb the ladder, muttering about that lazy boy. Guard lay still, trying hard to breathe as if he were asleep. His heart beat so fast he was afraid that Mr. Forrester would see it moving or even hear it beating.

A few minutes later, he heard the house door open, and then shut. As soon as he saw the bear oil lamps go out in the house, he slipped out the back of the barn.

Guard could not risk being seen by anyone, so he did not take the common trail to town. Instead he took a foot trail through the woods. It wasn't totally dark yet, and he was familiar with the area. This gave him a feeling of security.

He was so intensely involved in his thoughts that he didn't see all of the beauty surrounding him. The mountains far to the west were aglow in the rosy sunset. Any other time the lad would have spent a good long time gazing on this beauty of the distant hills.

Anxiously, he hurried over the tree roots and rocks, sometimes crawling on all fours trying to keep his balance. He wanted to hear everything Mr. Boone had to say. Guard stopped. He thought that he heard voices. This brought him suddenly back into reality. He quickly slouched down low behind a clump of mountain ivy.

In the glowing dusk he could see the form of a man and a woman coming from the trail leading from the river. No, it wasn't a woman. It was a girl just about his age. The sunset behind them gave a reddish glowing outline to their dark, shadowy forms.

"Yes, Daughter," the man said, "they say there's beaver, buffalo, turkey, deer, and lots of cleared land. They say that the long arm of King George can't reach us over the mountains. There'll be no tax collectors. Mr. Boone and the Long Hunters have been back and forth many times, and Matilda, my girl, we'd have our own land, and no English king could tell us what to do."

The slightly built girl was close enough now for Guard to see her. Her long golden hair framed a lovely face. She was about fourteen or fifteen years old. Her laughter was like the music of the branch as it broke over the rocks. "Oh, Pa, you speak like it is all settled and we're already over the mountains. Ye've not even heard Mr. Boone speak and give the details yet. Let's wait until we hear him before we make plans."

They passed on by him. It seemed to Guard that he had never seen anything or anyone so lovely. He was, at once, aware of his bare feet, his worn, homespun clothes, and his unkempt appearance. But just the remarks that he had overheard were enough to set his blood racing. Land far enough away from English Loyalists was land far enough away from Mr. Forrester. Did he dare go? Oh, he must hear Mr. Boone.

Mr. Boone was already speaking when Guard arrived. He stayed near the outer edge of the group, standing behind a tree. Boone was standing on the porch of the mercantile. Farmers were gathered all around. Guard strained to hear everything that the men were asking and what Mr. Boone was saying. He was afraid to move in closer, afraid that someone would see him and recognize him and tell Mr. Forrester.

"Yes, Gentlemen, there are Indians, but not right now, not in this area of the Watauga. They've just suffered a big defeat in war. They've moved farther west to their towns. These Indians are Cherokee. They are friendly and very talented. Their customs can be cruel, but they can be dealt with. I'm not saying that it's all peace. They can be troublesome. I've had some narrow escapes. I once hid under a waterfall and they didn't find me. Once I went into a cave and they followed me. But I found an opening in the top of it and I escaped. No...no, siree...it's not all easy. But it sure is a break from George. That's something to think about."

"Mr. Boone, are any white men over there already?" a man asked. Guard recognized Mr. Robertson as the man that Mr. Boone was looking for.

"Why, yes, Mr. Robertson, there are several Long Hunters here and there. These are mostly men who live in temporary shelters and hunt and trap. Now, down on the lower end of the Watauga River, near the same creek with the waterfall, there's a gentleman from Virginie, William Bean. Now, Mr. Bean, believe it or not, is of royal blood, but he moved down there to escape royal blood."

This remark brought laughter.

"Now, folks, jest think 'bout it...rich lands, plenty of game, clean water, few Indians, land jest fer the askin', no, I mean fer the workin'. I'm goin' back real soon, now. I'll mark a trail acrost the mountains, down Roany Creek, Doe River, and on down to the shoals on the Watauga."

The crowd broke up. Guard stood there caught up in his dreams. Dreams of owning his own land. Dreams of being free and of a home. He was slightly embarrassed to see in his dreams a blonde girl named Matilda. He was aware that the girl and her father were coming toward him. He stood there almost afraid to move. They might vanish. Her father lit a mullen-week torch. "Hurry along, Daughter, there be a little light left, but the woods will soon be dark, and this here torch won't last long. Gotta git home to yer ma. Don't want to worry her none."

Guard didn't move. Then, Matilda looked right at him and smiled.

Chapter Two

The morning broke, and so did the clouds. The rain came down in torrents. Guard didn't know whether to be glad or sad. The boy lay on the hay listening to the sound of the rain on the barn roof. He shivered in the cool dampness. The rain meant that the weeds would grow afresh. And this meant more back-breaking work without so much as a thank you. Work on someone else's land—but, Mr. Boone had said that there was land over the mountains. Free land, if a body was willing to work it.

Slowly he got up. Guard knew that rain wasn't enough to keep Mr. Forrester from finding work to do. He must report for duty. He climbed down the ladder and went out into the rain. He ran to the stoop. He didn't dare enter for fear that Mr. Forrester would curse him for dripping water on the puncheon floor.

"Git in here, Boy. What's the matter with ye? Git in here. I want ye to go to the settlement. Hit hain't gonna rain all day. We need some supplies. Take the sled and the mule. Git the skins to cover the goods. Don't linger all day, or I'll lay that one up with the rest, and then ye'll be getting one good 'un. Now listen up, and I'll tell ye what ye're to git. Ye mark it down...that's the only good thing about ye. Ye can make letters, and ye can cipher. Tell Mr. MacAfee to mark it down till I git in...now, listen up."

After writing down the things that Mr. Forrester wanted, Guard hurriedly harnessed the mule. He gathered skins and headed out into the blinding rain.

Shortly before reaching town the rain stopped, but the clouds were heavy and settled down low. They were so thick that he could not even see the mountains in the western distance. He always enjoyed watching the clouds as they rolled like silent waterfalls through the peaks, gaps, and hollows of the far away mountains. Now, however, it was all he could do to see the road as he came into the town.

A crowd was gathered at the mercantile. Among them was Mr. Robertson. He was stacking supplies on the counter.

"That's all I can take. That's about the limit my mules can carry. But I don't intend to be gone for too very long," he added. Men who sat around on boxes and barrels hung on every word.

"Well, Jim, ye're welcome to take my wagon if you'd like," one old man ventured.

"Sure would if I could, Zeb, but I'll do well to get there with two mules. There's no roads or trails wide enough for a wagon...just be me and the bears." Mr. Robertson laughed.

Guard walked over to the storekeeper and read him his list. It was times like this that made him feel important. That is—times when he read. Not many people could read. His ma had taught him. He could remember the fun and laughter when they had school. Mostly she had used the Bible, the Bible that Mr. Forrester had that was his.

After he read his list and the mercantile clerk got his supplies, he heard Mr. Robertson say, "Men, I'll be back as soon as I can. Don't know when. I just want to see for myself. If I like what I see, I may get set up for my family. Don't worry about the Indians. Mr. Boone says that they are at Chota. So unless I can't lick them bears, I'll be back. Then we'll make plans. One way or the other, we'll make plans. No one man, no king is going to tell me where I can or cannot go."

Guard surprised himself by thinking, "No king or no Mr. Forrester, either. That's my dream, but now, Mr. Forrester can tell me and does tell me what to do, and I'd best hurry or else."

Chapter Three

Several weeks passed. Crops were planted. Early producers were harvested. The days were long and hot.

Everywhere a group of men gathered together the talk turned to James Robertson. "When is he coming back?" "Is he dead?" "Was Boone wrong? Had the Indians gotten him?" "Did he meet up with a hungry bear?"

The corn was tasseling. Guard was in the field pulling weeds and suckers from around the corn. The stalks were almost as high as he. It was a nice looking patch. Guard wondered if it would be stealing if he put back a few grains of corn for seed. He'd need it on his land. Oh, here he was again, thinking about going over the mountains—making plans about what to do when he got there. Was he really going? Or was this just a dream that being an indentured boy fed?

He came to the end of the cornpatch. The stream was just over the embankment. He looked around for Mr. Forrester and then ran down the bank to get a quick drink of water. Guard stopped. It was James Robertson! He was back! He had gone over the mountains and he had returned! He was right there in front of Guard getting a drink of water!

Guard ran over eagerly. He was full of questions. "Mr. Robertson, you're back. The bears didn't get ye. Tell me what's it like over there? Are ya goin' back? Did ye see any Indians?"

"Whoa, Son, one question at a time. When I got there, I didn't find any Indians, but I did find some of their abandoned fields. I planted a garden and built a little cabin. And I am going back. I'm taking my family and anyone else who wants to go."

Through the next few days Guard kept his ears open. He listened to the men talk of supplies that they'd need. Things like iron tools, seeds, staples, things that would tide them over until they got to be self-sufficient. Everywhere he went he heard men talking. Even men who did not plan to go were talking about the necessities that would be useful.

If he went, how could he get supplies to take? He had no money, and nothing to barter. He had never been paid for all his work for Mr. Forrester. He hadn't even been well-fed, nor clothed properly. Would it be stealing if he took things? He wouldn't dare take any of Mr. Forrester's good tools, but if he happened to find anything just thrown away, discarded, he might take that.

Once again, he realized that he was talking to himself, making plans about going. Yes, he was going to go. He was! He was determined, but he needed to know more about it. And he needed to be ready when they decided to go. He knew that it would be soon. He had to find out without Mr. Forrester getting suspicious.

As Guard gathered in crops and worked around the barn, he put away seeds. He had beans, squash, corn, pumpkin, and even a few apple cores from the scrub apples he had taken from an old tree that no one cared for anymore. He carefully wrapped these in old cloths and labeled them.

One evening after Guard had gone to bed in the barn loft, and after Mr. Forrester had made a bed check, he remembered a place over in a ravine where trash had been thrown. Some of it was Mr. Forrester's, but some of it was already there, and had been for many years. Surely it wouldn't be stealing if he could find something there that he could use. He slipped out and climbed down into the ravine. He was glad that the moon was shining, and he seriously and prayerfully hoped that he wouldn't come across any snakes. After rummaging in it for a while, he found an old rusty ax-head. It was dull and had no handle, but he could use it. He would put it with his other things, and not sharpen it until he got there. Excitement filled him, and he kept hunting until he found an old piece of a knife. He would sharpen it now, because he might need it. He hunted awhile longer but found nothing else, so he went back to the barn loft.

Guard's big problem now was how to get some cooking

utensils, things like a spider (a cooking utensil with legs), or a fry pan. He'd just have to keep looking, and if he didn't find them, he would just do without.

As big as this problem seemed to him, he had another one that was causing him a lot of sadness. The only thing that he had left of his family's was his Ma's Bible, and Mr. Forrester had taken it to 'keep it safe fer him,' or so he had told Guard's mother. Guard knew better than to ask for it, or to even try and find it, but he did so want it. He just simply had to have it. A smile crept over his face as he remembered how his Ma had read the stories to them. This and the way that his Pa and his Ma had prayed about things were so much alive in his memory. But it had been such a long time since he had prayed. His life had been so lonely, so painful, that he felt that God had forgotten him, so why remind God now that he was still alive. Suddenly, it was so different, it was as if Ma was still alive and was standing there. Maybe God would be interested if he prayed about the Bible.

"Oh, God, effen you can heer me," he prayed in his mountain drawl, "I want my Ma's Bible. Can ye help me git it?" And then remembering how Ma had always ended her prayers, he added, "In Jesus' name, Forever, and ever, Amen."

It was just a few days later that things began to happen. Guard had picked up the ax and set out for the woodpile to cut kindling for the fireplace. As he approached the kitchen door with an armload of wood, he heard Mr. Forrester angrily talking to his wife, "Now, Maude, don't you let that thar boy find out 'bout all them folks here 'bouts makin' plans to go acrost the mountains. He might get fool idees in his head. We'd best keep an eye on him. And on them, too. I heerd Mr. Long from down on the river say that whenever they leave that they can't take much, so they'd jest leave what they can't take fer whoever finds it, and I'm gonna be the one that finds it, but fer now, I'm gonna go to town to find out all I can."

Guard quickly backed off without dropping the kindling in the woodbox beside the door. He wanted it to seem as if he were just walking up when Mr. Forrester came out, and sure enough he was able to do just that. As Mr. Forrester came out the door, he growled, "Boy, fill that box up and git the corn patch weeded 'fore dark. Let's see effen ye can earn yer salt fer a change."

Before Guard could answer, the man had ridden off toward town.

Mrs. Forrester was watching him ride off also. As soon as he was out of sight, she came out and spoke softly, "Thank you fer the wood."

"Yer welcome, Ma'm," he smiled at her. Her life wasn't very cheerful either. "Is there anything else I can do fer ye, Mrs. Forrester?"

"Why, yes, there is, Guard. My man has a book in there, a Bible, what fer I don't know. He can't read. If I fetch it, could ya read me jest a little of it? I don't get to meetin' much often, and I need to hear it read onct in a while. I never learnt to read none." The woman dropped her eyes shamedly.

Guard couldn't believe his ears. Could it be that God really did care for him...that He really had heard his prayers?

She went back into the little cabin and returned with the Bible, his Ma's Bible. "Here, read me about that shepherd that takes care of people."

"I will, effen I can find it. I hain't rightly familiar with the Book, Ma'm." His hands were shaking. "Let's see, here's that story 'bout a farmer sowing his field. Will hit do?"

He read a little of the story...his voice broke. His Ma seemed so near. He snapped back into reality and said, "Ma'm, I had best be gittin' to the cornfield. Effen you'd 'low it, I'd be obliged if I could take this Bible and study on it. I'll see effen I can find that story for ye."

Her face took on a scared look. She almost whispered. "I don't know...well, alright, if ye hide it. Don't let my man see it. And please don't say anything unless he is gone, please." Her eyes pleaded with him.

He hugged his mother's Bible to his heart, turned and ran into the barn. He hurried up the ladder to the loft, dug out a place in the hay, and lovingly placed it in the hollow he had made. Later he'd hunt a skin or a waterproof wrapping for it. He covered it up very carefully. This was really unbelievable. Five years had passed since he had seen this book. Five years since his mother had given this to him. Five years since she had placed him in indenture. Now, he had it again. And he meant to keep it. This wasn't stealing, this wasn't taking something that was not his. This Bible was his, his forever, and God had answered his prayers. God had not forgotten about him.

He scampered back down the ladder. His heart was light as he worked to get the field weeded before the darkness fell. He finished weeding the corn patch just as the twilight's rosy glow crept over the mountainous horizon. As he neared the cabin from the corn patch he saw Mr. Forrester ride in from town and enter the cabin. His heart began to beat fiercely. He just had to find out what the man had learned in town. Silently, Guard slipped around behind the cabin. He knew that eavesdropping was wrong, but he just had to know.

"Yes, Maude," he heard him saying. "They're goin' the day after 'morrow, come first light. They start gatherin' in the settlement tomorrow and leave out next mornin', headin' west. I, fer one, say 'good riddance'... hain't no good'll come out of it. Soon's they get gone, I'm headin' out to get me some house plunder. I heered Long say he'd move his family out tomorrow. He says he's just goin' to leave anything he can't take. Suits me jest fine. I'll go down river 'bout daylight next day and see what I can git."

Guard went to the woodpile, gathered up an armload of wood, and carried it to the woodbox. He made noise as he came upon the stoop. He wanted to make sure that they heard him.

The noise of the wood rolling into the woodbox brought a string of oaths from Mr. Forrester. Guard scarcely heard the violent torrent. His mind was too busy making plans.

He quietly took the supper that Mrs. Forrester handed him and carried it back to the barn. Once within the barn, he got his Ma's Bible, now carefully wrapped in a dry raccoon hide, along with his rusty ax head and his only extra shirt. He rolled them into a tight bundle. Within the bundle he slipped the seeds that he had stashed back. He looked toward the house. Everything looked fine, so he slipped out into the woods behind the barn. He stuck his precious bundle back into a washed out hole under a root ledge. He covered it with leaves and hurried back to the barn loft. He put his bearskin cover where he could quickly get it when he left.

Guard had just lain down when Mr. Forrester entered the barn. He climbed the ladder. Guard faked sleep and Mr. Forrester left.

There wasn't much sleep for the seventeen year old orphan that night. He remembered the good times with Pa, Ma, and his brother Garse. He lay there wondering where his brother was now. Garse, who was a year older than Guard, had been bound out to a preacher-man, that was all he knew. But he couldn't worry about that now. He must concentrate on his plans for leaving.

Mr. Forrester was unusually mean the next day. Nothing Guard did pleased him. He stayed in the field with him all day, as if he were watching him. Guard worked without stopping for food or water. But, today, his heart was light, and nothing could bother him. Several times, Mr. Forrester struck Guard across the shoulders with a small tree limb. Once he even spit tobacco juice on Guard's feet, all the while muttering vile things about the bonded lad.

It was almost dark when they returned from the field. Guard washed up in the rain barrel and went to get his supper. Mr. Forrester was very busy eating and didn't notice that his wife had slipped extra corn pone and fried side meat to Guard.

This extra kindness took him by surprise. "Do you reckon she knows?" he thought. "Of course not. There was no way. Maybe she was hoping that he would go. Well, anyway, this extra food would come in handy. He'd save it for later on. But for now he would just eat some scrubby apples."

After bedcheck, Guard slipped out. He checked his Bible and other supplies. With them he put some raw vegetables, things he would eat as he traveled. Mr. Forrester had said that the Long's cabin was down on the river. That meant downstream. He just knew that he would find the cabin.

After about an hour and a half, Guard came to a cabin. It looked deserted, but he called out. When there was no answer, he went in. It was obvious that the occupants were gone. He let his eyes get accustomed to the darkness. He could now distinguish shapes. He crawled around on the floor. His hand hit a heavy iron pot. It was a spider, which is a rather flat pan on legs, to be used over an open fire. He continued to feel around the cabin. On the fireboard above the fireplace, he found a handleless cup.

He heard a sound. Someone or something was coming. Could it be that Mr. Forrester had followed him? There was no place to hide. He quickly got behind the door. It was being pushed open. It was a dog, a big, red hound dog. He stood breathless. Even a dog, especially a strange one, could be vicious. He waited. The dog approached. He didn't bark, nor growl. Instead he whined. Guard spoke gently, "Here, boy, nice boy." The dog came over and rubbed his wrinkled skin against Guard's leg. Guard breathed a sigh of relief. He sat down on the floor and began petting the dog, talking gently to him. By now, the moon was rising, letting more light into the cabin. He looked around. In the corner on a hook, he saw a rather large piece of a linsey-woolsey coverlet. This was just what he needed, a covering. He could, also, tie up his house plunder in it. He placed his plunder into this piece of fabric, tied the corners, and slipped out into the night. The red hound followed him, dragging a rawhide rope.

Guard tried to drive the dog back. But his sad look and pitiful whine tore at his heart. The dog was just like he was, wanting freedom and companionship. He just couldn't leave him.

He took the plunder and hid it with the other things. He thought of the dog and his own loneliness when he tied him up about a mile up in the woods away from the Forrester's cabin. He had taken him far off the trail that Mr. Forrester would use the next morning as he went to the Long's cabin, for he had no place to keep the dog or to hide him if he brought him back.

Guard had decided to give the Robertson party a full day's head start, then he would leave. He knew that as soon as Mr. Forrester missed him that he would go the first thing to the Robertson party to see if he were with them. He wouldn't be, but he would be near by. For three or four days he planned to move in the same direction but far enough away for them not to see him. He'd give Mr. Forrester plenty of time to come looking and be satisfied that he was not with them before he joined them.

Chapter Four

The boy and dog, which he called "Red," became fast friends. Together, on this night in late summer, 1771, they traveled deep into the woods. Guard knew the general direction. But right now, he was so grateful for the dog. He knew the hound would lead him right to his master whenever the time was right. He was trusting in the dog to be faithful.

Each day for three days they moved at a safe distance from the Robertson party. Travel was slow going up the mountain. There was no trail to follow along this part of the mountain. On the third day of their trip, Guard tied Red to a tree about a half mile away and slipped in closer. Red had caught a rabbit that afternoon, and was just finishing it up. Guard hoped that he would soon be asleep and not give him away with his baying.

The boy edged in as closely as he could. He could see a campfire burning in a cleared spot about ten feet away. For the first time he realized that he was cold. It was much colder on these high mountains than in the low country he had just left. He had not been prepared for the chilly air. Even if he had known it would be so cool, he didn't have any warm clothes to bring with him. He shivered and looked longingly at the warmth of the fire.

And...as he looked, he saw her...the golden haired girl from the woods. She was walking from behind two oxen, and was heading for the warmth of the fire.

A kind faced woman spoke to her softly, "Now, Tildy, don't grieve so. We'll get another dog someday." She had such a kind voice. A kindness he hadn't heard since his Ma died. She continued, "Your dog has been found by now. There's surely been someone by there by now who's found him."

"I know, Ma, but I miss King so much. He was my dog. I've

had him since he was just a pup. I love him."

Guard gasped. Why had he not made the connection? That night in the woods they had entered from the river road by the creek, he knew that they were going. But he didn't know their names. What would they think when he showed up with their dog and their house plunder?

The barefoot boy crawled over through the edge of the woods to another campfire. "Whatcha reckon happened to Forrester's indentured boy? When he came by here yesterday he didn't act like he believed us when we told him that we hadn't seen him. Wouldn't of told him if I had known. A body hain't got no business treating another body the way he did that boy, don't care if he did own him," one old man said.

The other man aimed his tobacco juice at the dying fire. He spoke slowly, "Don't rightly know, but can't say as I blame the boy. Myself, fer one, hain't got no use fer Forrester, not now, nor never."

"Who was that there boy, anyhow?" the first man asked.

"Don't know...just called him Guard," was the answer. "But I onct heerd that he was the grandson of a family named McCall from down on the Piedmont. Heerd his grand-pap disowned his pappy when he left and married. Said he married 'neath him."

Hot tears burned his eyes. His Pa and his Ma had never talked about their families. And Ma hadn't made any effort to get in touch with any of Pa's family when Pa died and she needed help.

He stood up to move back up the mountain. It was dark now and they wouldn't see him. But the aroma of frying sidemeat penetrated his nostrils. His head began to swim. Everything was moving.

A cool hand was on his brow. He tried to move. "Ma," he said.

"Sh-h, Son, how long has it been since you've had a decent meal?" A kind, motherly, voice was speaking.

He tried to speak, but he couldn't. He was shivering, and was too weak to speak.

He knew that someone was trying to feed him some broth. "Here, taste a little of this broth from our supper. It's rabbit stew."

He swallowed a little of the broth, and after resting awhile longer, he was able to eat some more.

"You're Forrester's boy, aren't you?" she asked softly.

"Yes, I am." Soon he heard himself telling them his story. When he got to the part about going to their cabin and about the dog, he heard a gasp.

"King. Where is he?"

Guard sat up and pointed as he spoke. "I wasn't stealin', was I? I didn't mean to steal, honest. Yer dog is tied 'bout half mile up that way. I couldn't a done without him." He laughed a little short laugh. "I called him 'Red.' I figgered he'd lead me to you all's party. He'd a come to ya anytime I turned him to it. He's up there with my pack." He started to get up.

"Oh, no, yer not, you jest stay right there," Mr. Long said firmly. "I'll go. I'll find him. If I git up there on that mountain and whistle, he'll answer me. Fer now, let's jest thank the good Lord that yer all right. He took care of ye up on that mountain alone. I'll git someone to go with me."

After Mr. Long left, Mrs. Long said, "Guard, you need rest and we're heading out tomorrow, so you just lie still. I'll get some covers. You need to keep warm. Nights get pretty chilly up here on these mountains." No one had been this kind to him since his mother died. This woman didn't even know him, yet she was so kind. He didn't know how to react, so he answered, "I'm fine, Ma'm. I've got a bear skin in my pack. I can use that."

But she insisted. She sent Matilda for the coverlet and also for her Bible. She moved over near the fire to get what little bit of light there was left from it. She opened the Bible and read from it.

The Lord is my shepherd; I shall not want.
He maketh me to lie down in green pastures:
He leadeth me beside the still waters....

When she had finished, he quietly spoke to her, "I've got a Bible. It's in my pack. And I can read it. My Ma taught me. When she left, she gave me her Bible."

And once again, he found himself telling them another chapter of his story. He told them about how he got the Bible from the Forresters. When he finished he asked her, "Ma'm, was I stealing? It was really mine."

"No, Son, you weren't stealing. God just gave you back what you'd lost and what you needed. That's the kind of God we serve. Now before we retire, let's pray."

They bowed and she prayed. "Dear Lord, thank You for lending Your protectin' hand to us this day, and for protectin' this here young man. Continue to be with us as we cross these mountains to our new home. Provide us with knowledge to learn Your Word. Protect Mr. Long in the mountains. In Jesus' name, Amen."

Under his breath Guard spoke, "Forever and ever...Amen."

Chapter Five

The next few days were exciting. Never had the pioneers seen such beauty. Huge rocks jutted from the tops and sides of great high mountains. Creeks and rivers cascaded over boulders larger than any Guard had ever seen. The shadows outlined the far mountains. Every ridge and crest was accented against the clear blue of the skies.

He was standing near the edge of a cliff looking out over the far off mountains. Matilda came up softly and stood quietly beside him. She pointed to a ridge far beyond them across a valley. "Look," she whispered reverently. "Looks like punched down bread dough. God musta punched down the valleys and pushed up the mountains. Those must be God's fingerprints in the dough."

He started to speak. She placed her finger on his lips whispering, "Sh-h." Her eyes said, "Don't break the spell." They stood watching a river far off in the distance, winding snakelike in and out of the vales and gorges. Far off, an eagle soared on an updraft. In the valley far below them, deer playfully scampered.

She spoke very softly, "And God said, 'Let there be hills, valleys, eagles, rivers, and let there be...'" she stopped, looked up at him and smiled. "Let there be...us." Her eyes twinkled, she turned around, and hurried back.

He watched her go. He enjoyed being near her. She was so happy, so full of life, and she was so gentle and kind. Like today, when she offered to carry the Blevins's baby awhile so the mother could rest. Sometimes she gathered all the children around her. As they walked she would play games with them. Games like, "I See." Sometimes she would sing ditties with them, like, "Coming Through the Rye," or "This Way and That Way."

Guard busied himself with helping the men guide the oxen and the milch cows down the trails. These trails wound up and down, in and out, around and around to the base of each rising. He felt like it took them ten miles for each mile "as the crow flies." Tired, but happy, Guard was enjoying his freedom. Yet, deep within him was a constant fear that just anytime he might look up and see Mr. Forrester there.

One afternoon, Mr. Robertson, who was leading the caravan, stopped and called back, "We'll camp on that bald spot down there." He pointed to a grassy knoll below them. "It looks like rain to the southeast, and if I remember correctly, there's a ledge under which we can wait out the storm. Let's move on and get there before the storm hits."

They arrived at the cliff shelter just as the rainstorm hit. The wind and the rain were violent. The rain swept over them in torrential waves. Since they had no way to build fires or to prepare food, they huddled as far as possible under the ledge both for warmth and protection.

A lull in the wind allowed another sound to reach the ears of Mr. Long. He raised his eyebrows and looked at Mr. Blevins. They both looked at Guard. The look on their faces told him to be quiet and not panic and alarm the women and children, but to move out of there immediately.

Guard looked at Matilda. She was embracing a small girl wrapped in her cloak. Both were almost asleep. He touched her arm. She looked up at him sleepily. He mouthed silently, "Move over here," motioning with his head.

Her facial expression asked, "Why?" But she moved out without waiting for an answer. She noticed that her mother and Mrs. Blevins were already over near the front edge. Silently and quickly she went with Guard, carrying the drowsy child.

Guard mouthed silently, "Rattlesnakes."

Just then the little girl awoke and began crying, "My doll. I want my doll."

Without thinking, Guard ran back to get the doll.

"No, Guard, no," Matilda called in a frightened voice.

Her warning came too late. His bare feet made an inviting target for the large, coiled rattlesnake. Just as it sprang,

Guard was knocked out of the way by a tree branch wielded by Mr. Long. The branch then came down rapidly on the snake. Stunned, Guard stood motionless. Mr. Long walked over and picked up the dead, though squirming snake.

Guard felt embarrassed, but grateful. Mr. Long scolded him, and said, "It is of the good Lord's merciful providence, Son, fer this we are eternally thankful. Seven rattles and a button. That's not to be taken lightly. Least we know that we're coming down, we're below the snake line."

The lad blushed and trembled with delayed fear. He couldn't speak, not yet.

"Now, listen, Son," Mr. Long said, as he placed a strong arm around Guard's shoulder. "Been givin' it considerable thought. You need a family and I need help. Tildy, there, she can't cut down trees. Why, she can't even swing an ax." He winked lovingly at his daughter. "You jest hang 'round with us and we'll give ye room and board, till ye git set up on your own...know ye want freedom, and ye've got it. Leave anytime...and there'll be none of that servant stuff. We'll jest be two men, equal...think it over."

Guard started to answer, but Mr. Long stopped him. "Not yet, Son. Now, we've got rules, though, me and my missus. We're Bible believing Christians. Don't allow no drinking, cursing, profanity 'round us. My missus, she reads the Good Book to us. Sometimes Tildy reads it. We'll treat ye fair and square.

"Now there's 'nother thing, too dangerous 'out no shoes. Here's a pair one of the fellows give me fer ye. Looks too big, but we'll put some fur in the toes. Later, we can get a pair what fits."

Guard's eyes were wet. He wasn't used to kindness. Mr. Long didn't have to worry none about his drinking and cursing. He'd seen too much of that from Mr. Forrester, enough to last him a lifetime.

The rain stopped. A heavy fog was settling in on the mountain. The sun was shining through the mist. It gave an almost ethereal aura to the knoll. Guard looked at Matilda. She was looking at him. Her eyes smiled. She quickly looked down and blushed.

"I'm glad you didn't get bitten," she said. "If you had, you might of died."

"Well, I am too. I should've known better. I've killed a few of them myself back over the mountains. I know that them things are deadly."

Saying these words, 'over the mountains,' made him realize that he had crossed over to forbidden land. The king of England had given orders that no one was to cross the ridge, sometimes called the watershed. Everyone knew why. He wanted his tax collectors to get all the money that they could from the settlers. It was hard enough to collect money from the backwoodsmen east of the ridge in North Carolina. They weren't going to want to come over here and face all these dangers just to collect taxes.

Freedom, that's the reason that they all came! Freedom. Guard was doubly free...twice freed. Free from George III, and free from Mr. Forrester. The thrill of it ran through him and he shivered. He raised his arms and sang out, "Matilda, I'm free." He wanted to grab her and twirl her around...but he didn't.

Chapter Six

It was almost noon the next day before the fog burnt off and they could move on. Even cooking was difficult. The clouds were so low that they held the smoke and made breathing a problem. So they ate cold corn cakes and packed up.

"Tildy." Mrs. Long said, "Take this basket and keep your eyes open for 'salet' greens as we walk. I've seen some nice, tender, green shoots along the way. High as we are, there'll still be some young and tender ones growing. See, there's some 'poke salet.' When we make camp tonight, we'll cook 'em. I'll check the hen cages and see if there's any eggs. Be a good treat fer us, and good fer us too."

Mrs. Long went to check the two hen cages that were strapped to the flanks of the oxen. Matilda took the basket. Guard walked with her. The flat land along the side of the creek was grassy and cool. Salad greens were plentiful. Guard spotted some that even Matilda wasn't familiar with. They gathered wild mustard, dandelion, dock, thistle, poke, lambs quarter, and even blackberry leaves. Then he spotted a large area of field creasies. Some had already gone to seed, but he searched until he found some tender ones. He picked them and carried them to her. As he put them in her basket his hand touched hers. The color rose in her face. "Thank you," she spoke softly.

When they made camp later on that evening, Mr. Long took some twigs and vines and fashioned a fish trap. "An Indian trap," he said. "Fish and salet will sure be tasty tonight."

Several of the other men had fashioned fish traps. Soon the air was filled with the tantalizing aroma of frying fish. Even King was overcome with excitement.

"Howdy, folks, that'll be fish I smell, I reckon?"

They looked up to see a man in buckskins, Indian moccasins, and a coonskin cap approaching the camp. He was dragging a travois packed with furs. He carried a long rifle over his shoulder and a powder horn.

He looked around the camp and shouted, "Well, effen hit hain't my old friend, James Robertson. If ya hain't a sight fer sore eyes. I figgered effen ye's coming back a'tall, hit'd be 'bout now."

Mr. Robertson clasped the man and laughed. This was one of the Long Hunters who had saved his life last spring. He never thought that he'd ever see him again. "Come on, join us, stay long as you like. Folks, here's one of the hunters who nursed me to health when I got lost on this same mountain. Storm about like that one yesterday...where you heading?"

"Goin' over to Salem. Got ary messages fer folks over that away?" the hunter asked.

Guard froze. What if someone sent a message to Mr. Forrester that he was with the Robinson party. What if the Long Hunter ran into Mr. Forrester on the way? What if Mr. Forrester asked questions? Guard slipped over next to the edge of the woods. Perhaps the fur trader wouldn't see him. He tried to be inconspicuous.

Mr. Long watched him. He walked over to him. "Don't do this, Son. This makes you obvious. Jest act normal. Don't overdo hit, one way or 'tother. Stay near us. 'Sides, hain't nobody here gonna give ye 'way. We all prize our freedom too much to take yours away from you."

The fear Guard felt lessened, but not completely. Would he never be free from this nagging fear?

Mr. Long continued, "We'll pray 'bout it. Let's ask the Almighty to do what has to be done. He knows best."

Matilda came over to tell them that supper was ready. Her Pa left them and went on back to the fire and to supper, leaving them alone.

"Don't let it get you down, Guard. We just live one day at a time. Come on, let's go eat them salet greens."

After supper, he unrolled his bearskin, carefully placing his Ma's Bible in the folds for protection. He wrapped up in the bearskin. He was tired and sleepy, but sleep did not come. He lay awake far into the night. Did he do wrong to leave Mr. Forrester? Was he obliged to stay with him longer? Ma had told him that he only had to stay for five years. But Mr. Forrester had said it was seven years. That left two years. Should he go back? If it was seven years, what should he do? Legally he wasn't free. He was bound!

Although he was restless and troubled, he felt peace and joy, all this at one time. He didn't understand it. He'd never known any people as kind as the Longs. And even the other people had gone out of their way to help him. They seemed to understand. He felt a kinship of spirit with them...a spirit of freedom. Even the black man that one of them owned was not treated as a slave. They all knew the value of freedom.

And Matilda...such a musical name. He could never call her Tildy. Her name was musical...her golden hair and her green eyes...her laughter. As sleep came upon him, Matilda changed to Ma. In his dreams Ma was standing in front of him. She was reading his Bible to him.

Early the next morning Guard began to pack up his belongings. He arranged his seeds, placing them and his mother's Bible in the bear skin, getting ready to roll them up. But for some reason, he opened the Bible. He didn't know why. Maybe it just brought him a little closer to Ma. The Bible fell open. It opened to a paper wedged deep into the spine. He removed it. It was faded and creased. It had been there a long time. In the early light he began to read. It was the contract his Ma had made with Mr. Forrester, and read, "five year's servitude."

He was free, really free! Guard McCall was free.

"Mr. Long! Mrs. Long! Matilda! King! Everybody! I'm free! Looka here, I'm free! Praise the Lord, I'm free!"

Everyone came running. Guard was dancing and yelling, laughing and crying all at once. Everyone was talking at once, and trying to find out what was happening. After finally calming down, Guard told them about his fear of being still legally bound to Mr. Forrester. He told them that Mr. Forrester said that he had two more years to serve. But here was the proof. He was free.

Mr. Long spoke up, "I think that it's fittin' that we thank the Almighty. I told you, Guard, that the Almighty would take over if ye'd let Him."

After Mr. Long prayed, he said, "Tildy, after we eat our breakfast, why don't ye and Guard take the skillets and pots down to the creek bank and clean 'em up. We'll be headin' out soon's we eat our grub and pack up."

They knelt on the creek bank in the sand and scrubbed the bake oven and the spider with a piece of sandstone that they found there. Guard spoke first, "Matilda, I can't thank you all 'nuff fer helpin' me. Hain't no one's ever been so good to me since my Ma died. Matilda, did God really do this fer me?"

"Why, yes, Guard, I believe that He did. He cares for us all. He'll do great things for us if we let Him." She smiled up at him.

He reached over and got hold of her hand. He held it for a few seconds. "Thank you," he said softly. Then, all the color drained from his face. He was ashen white, as if scared. "Matilda, let me tell you about the very first time I ever saw you." Then Guard told her about that night in the woods as he was slipping into town to hear Daniel Boone tell about the Overmountain Country. He told her about the sunset behind her in the woods, giving her such a lovely rosy glow.

She stood listening, tears were on her dark eyelashes, framing her lovely green eyes. She leaned over and kissed him. Then she picked up a clean pan and turned to return to the camp. "We'd better hurry. They'll be ready to move out." She spoke very softly.

Soon the wild rugged mountain was behind them. A small roaring river tumbled rapidly down to the valley below. It wound around through rocks and gorges, sometimes deep, and sometimes wide and shallow, right at land level. It seemed to be thriving with fish. Wild flowers bloomed along the banks. Here and there were cleared fields. Guard thought that they must be some the Indians had cleared and left.

He heard Mr. Long call out, "Robertson, we 'bout there? Seems like a lot of flat land 'round here."

"Not yet, Mr. Long. Be there by dark. That's not the Watauga. It is just a tributary of the Watauga, the Doe. Watauga's much bigger. Won't be long now."

Just knowing that they were almost there gave them extra energy. Although they knew that much hard work was ahead, they let their spirits rest in the secure feeling of being home. No cabins yet and no gardens, but they had freedom. It was home.

It wasn't much longer till they arrived at the "Old Fields," beside a wide river. Robertson called the small group together. "Well, folks, we're here. Let's thank the Lord for His protection. Mr. Long, will you lead us?"

All the men removed their hats and knelt on the mossy ground. The children stood quietly. The women breathed soft prayers and cried softly. The Watauga River gently sang as it moved to meet the Holston farther west.

"Father, we bow our heads in gratitude for your guidance and protection during our trip. The elements did not conquer us. The animals did not attack us. We suffered no great loss other than a few supplies. We're here to do yer biddin', to honor and worship ye, as free men. We ask for yer further guidance and protection. Be with us as we gather foodstuffs for the coming winter. Be with us as we build our cabins. Thank ye, Lord, Amen."

The other men echoed, "Amen."

And Guard said, "Forever and ever...Amen." He spoke it very softly.

Chapter Seven

Guard leaned on his plow handles. While he rested for a few minutes, he thought over the last few months. This past winter had been hard. The men had formed teams as soon as they had arrived to help each other. They had built the cabins quickly. As soon as the first ones were finished the women and the children had moved in. It was cramped, but in just a short time other cabins were ready. During the daytime, the women and children worked on getting the gardens ready for what food could be planted this late. It was a gamble, but if the weather cooperated there might be some late corn and beans. They had gathered all the wild edibles that they could find. The children had searched diligently for good river rocks for their fireplaces and chimneys. They had hunted for good veins of clay for mortar to chink the logs. They had quickly learned to use the clay. There was always a task to be done and someone to do it, no matter how young or old. Everyone worked and helped each other.

The winter was hard and costly. A graveyard was already begun. In it were buried a mother and her newborn infant. Some of the women were grief-stricken because the baby who had lived only a few days had not been baptized. Guard could not understand. What did they mean? Surely God would not doom an innocent infant who had had no chance to live. Whenever he could he was going to ask Matilda about it.

He pushed his red hair out of his eyes, and began to plow again. He hoped his seeds would grow. He had beans, corn, pumpkins, and squash. He had saved these seeds until this spring for planting. He had his own field. Mr. Robertson had allowed him to select a piece of land, just like the other men with families. He was late, though, in getting his crops in the ground because he had wanted to help Mr. Long before he began his own. Sometimes Mr. Long had helped him, but he wanted to do it by himself. He wanted to prove something to himself and to the others. He wanted to prove that he could shoulder responsibility like a man. And then...maybe...just maybe, if he were successful and got a cabin raised, Matilda might agree to marry him.

His thoughts meandered over many things. Mr. Robertson had told them that others would be coming, some were even coming from Virginia. Maybe there would be a preacher-man, and then....

Guard was sure that Matilda felt like he did. He just knew that she did. He had never mentioned this to her, but he just knew that she cared. They spent a lot of time together, and they laughed a lot. Once he had kissed her.

He was busy plowing and throwing out clumps of grass from the rich soil. He didn't see Matilda as she ran up. She called out breathlessly, "Hurry, Indians! Run to the fort!"

He left his plow and together they ran into the open fort, through gates that he had helped build. Others were hurrying in. His heart beat rapidly. Indians! He'd seen Indians before, but not on their grounds, not in the wilderness.

Mr. Robertson quickly sent the women and children into safer quarters. All the men took their prearranged posts.

A small group of Indians approached the fort at Sycamore Shoals. They were not wearing warpaint, but were carrying furs. After a time of trial and error communications by James Robertson, it was established that they weren't hostile. They were seeking food supplies, scouting for buffalo, and other game. The winter had been equally hard on them in their overhill town of Chota. Many braves had died in the recent war with the Chickamaugas and crops had been destroyed. The Indians wanted food for their party, any foods that could be spared, and seeds. For this they would give furs. The exchange was made and the braves left.

Mr. Robertson called the settlers together. "Folks, today seemed harmless enough, and it may well have been, but we must always be on the lookout for trouble. They saw more than we realize here. We must remember, however, that if we can keep an active friendship between the Cherokee and us, we will stand a better chance."

Not long after this, Guard completed his cabin and then two things happened: Mr. Robertson had a visitor, and the men had a conference.

"This is Mr. Bean. He's from over near Boone's Creek. He tells me that several other settlers have come in. There are groups in several places. We've invited the leaders from each of these settlements to meet with us. We need rules. We need regulations. We must establish laws. It stands to reason that if honest, God-fearing people move in here to escape the tyranny of George III, then dishonest men will come to escape honest punishment. We must plan ahead.

"The other thing I must tell you is more serious than I thought. We are not in Virginia as we thought. We are on the part of the Granville Claim; land that North Carolina grant office has closed. In other words, we are on Cherokee land. We are on their hunting ground. As soon as possible some of us will have to go treaty with the Indians."

After a few more minutes of discussion, it was agreed that Mr. Robertson and William Bean's son, John, would travel to Chota to visit with the Indians and work out a settlement.

After the meeting was over, Guard walked over to the Long's cabin with Mr. Long. "Howdy, Son," said Mrs. Long, "Yer gonna eat tonight with us, I do hope."

"Yes'm, I will," he answered eagerly. Things were looking up for him. This might be a good chance to talk to Matilda. So after supper he said, "Matilda, let's help yer ma out. Let's take her iron pots down to the creek bank and scrub them out good fer her."

They carried the heavy pots down the path to the creek. The cabin roof was barely visible from their working area. Guard set the heavy black pots down. Matilda knelt down to begin scrubbing them. Her golden hair had been pulled back behind her ears, Indian style. Guard reached over and got her by the hand.

"Matilda, my cabin is 'most done. My crops are planted. Even my apple tree seeds have sprouted. My cabin still hain't got no floor, but I promise to floor it as soon as I can...Matilda, will ye marry me? We could get married as soon as a preacher-man comes by here."

Guard was breathless. Tears were spilling over his sun-tanned face. "I love you. I've loved you since that first time I saw you, there in the woods. I'll take care of ye, Matilda. Will ye? Please say, 'Yes.'"

Matilda was trembling. Color had drained from her face. Tears were spilling over her long lashes to her cheeks.

"Don't cry...don't cry. I'm sorry," Guard whispered.

She spoke with a trembling voice. "Don't be sorry. You've done nothing wrong. I love you, too. I think I always have. Yes, I'll marry you. But, Guard, you must go ask Pa."

Guard gathered her close to his chest. He kissed her gently. "Ye'll never be sorry. I promise you."

They started back up the small hill. At the same time they said, "The pots. We forgot the pots."

They ran back to the creek bank and quickly scrubbed the iron pots. They laughed and splashed water like two small children.

Mr. Long was sitting outside the cabin. He was painstakingly sharpening a sickle on a hone-stone. "Guard, is that there ax head of yourn holdin' an edge? Bring it over and I'll work on hit some more."

Guard didn't answer him. He and Matilda carried the freshly scrubbed pots back into the cabin. A few minutes later Guard came out.

"Mr. Long, would ya like to see my apple trees? Never dreamed that that many of 'em would sprout. Them was jest cores left from the scrub apples I brought to eat on the way. May be that we can transplant some of 'em up here."

Mr. Long laid down his sickle and hone. They walked down the path toward Guard's small one-room cabin. The apple trees were visible and recognizable a few inches above the ground.

Mr. Long stopped and looked at Guard, "What is it, Son? Ye got a problem?"

"Well, no, Sir, yes, Sir—yes, I do. It's only a problem effen I let it to be. Sir, I want to marry Matilda. I hain't got much, but I do love her. I'll never do her nothin' but proud. Sir, can ye give us your blessin'?" Guard stopped for breath.

Mr. Long stopped. He cleared his throat, pulled a blade of grass from its sheath, and began chewing on it. "Son, I've been 'spectin' this. Can't honestly say that they's anybody else that I'd want to see her marry. Ye know that she's all we got, and we jest can't be too careful. But ye've got my blessin'. Now, when is this here weddin' gonna happen?"

Guard was so excited that he could hardly answer. "Don't know, Sir, gotta do it up right. Whenever a preacher-man comes by, I guess. Mr. Robertson said that it could be any day now. Might be one'll come when they gather to organize a government. Think I'll ask Mr. Robertson to inquire about a preacher-man effen he stops at the other settlements when he visits the Indian towns, that is, effen one don't come first."

He grabbed the older man's hand, " Thank you, Sir, thank you. Gotta go...gotta go tell Matilda."

Before the party left for Chota, the leaders of the various settlements gathered to organize the new government. It was in May of 1772, when the first free government in America, independent of any other state or colony, was formed. The commissioners of the newly formed Watauga Assembly were representative of all the forts or areas of settlement located "over the mountains." John Carter, James Robertson, Charles Robertson, Zachariah Isbell, and probably Jacob Brown formed this group. One of their responsibilities was to issue marriage licenses. They also authorized James Robertson to perform marriage ceremonies.

As soon as Guard heard about this, he immediately took out a marriage license for himself and Miss Matilda Long. He wanted to be ready as soon as Mr. Robertson returned from Chota.

During the weeks that Robertson and John Bean were gone to the Indian towns, Matilda and Guard planned and prepared. So many things had to be done. She and her mother picked and dried berries and beans, smoked and dried meat, and anything else that could be put up for winter.

Mrs. Bean on one of her rare trips to Sycamore Shoals had taught the women about the native plants that were edible, and about herbs that could be used for medicines. Matilda had dried wild cherry bark, goldseal, bloodroot, and other medicines. She had also started an herb garden beside the little cabin that was soon to be her home.

A group of fur traders came by on their way to the trading posts across the mountains, back in Carolina. Guard had a sizable pile of furs ready for trading. He sent them by these traders to trade for some of the necessities that would be needed in their new home. Among these things that he sent for were a wedding ring and some material for Matilda to make herself a new dress.

The crops were doing as well as he expected, it being the first crop on this new ground. There would be enough for them to make it until the following spring.

Guard dug a pit with a small enclosure for smoking deer and bear meat. He also prepared bear fat for soap and candle making. He built a spring house over a little spring which ran through his fields toward the river. But first, he dug out a place to put some of his squash and pumpkins and someday his apples. No, *their* apples. He mustn't forget. Not his, but theirs.

Before Colonel Robertson (as he was now called) returned, the group of Long Hunters, or fur traders, came back into the settlement. Guard was surprised that they had been gone such a short time, and relieved that they were honest.

The Long Hunters had brought him back some seed potatoes. It was too late to plant them this year. But he decided to plant a few, just to see what they would make. The rest he would store until next spring. If he needed them he would use them for food. He placed the potatoes in a nest of dried grass in the dugout part of the spring house. He knew that it was risky, and he would have to keep the eyes cleaned off. He figured that they would be tempting to small animals, and they might even freeze, but he'd take the chance.

Among the supplies that the Long Hunters brought back to him was a bolt of calico, just the color of Matilda's eyes. He couldn't wait to surprise her with it.

And they also brought a wedding ring!

Chapter Eight

Colonel Robertson and John Bean had a very successful trip to the Indian towns, and to celebrate, the Indians were invited to visit their settlement. Settlers were coming in from all directions around the Watauga Assembly. All the member forts of the Assembly were to be there.

Matilda and Guard decided that this would be a good time for their wedding. Her calico dress was almost finished. It just needed a few touches here and there on it. This was to be her wedding dress.

The day finally arrived. The flat river bottom land was teeming with activity. Venison was roasting on many of the campfires scattered around the valley. Near-naked Indians were roaming around the cabins. Often they would just walk into a cabin unannounced, but the settlers tried to be patient with them, so as not to cause any friction or problems during the days that they would be there.

Toward noon, Mr. and Mrs. Robertson, by pre-arranged plan, came to the Long's cabin. Guard met Mr. Robertson outside. In his hands he carried his Ma's Bible. "Colonel Robertson, Sir, would ye do me proud and read from my Ma's Bible today?" He handed it to Col. Robertson, who opened it to the front. As his eyes read the handwritten family history written there, his facial expression changed.

"Josh McCall! You...Josh McCall's son?"

"Ya knew my Pa? Tell me, you knew my Pa?" Guard asked puzzlingly.

"Yes, Guard, your Pa was a friend of mine, a childhood friend. It's been years...I just never dreamed. I'm sorry about your misfortune in life...but I am glad that you are with us."

Colonel Robertson read on. "See here that he married Sarah Thomason. I knew her, too. Hum-m...you've got a brother,

Garse. Where is he?"

"Don't know, Sir. I'd sure like to know. He was bound out to a preacher-man. I heerd it was one of them Anabaptists down in Carolina. I've never given up hope that someday I'll find him."

Robertson smiled, "Well, this day doesn't call for tears, but for happiness. Let's get to this wedding and then continue on in our celebration."

He read from Guard's mother's Bible. He chose the verses from the Book of Ruth. "Whither thou goest, I will go," he read. Soon the ceremony was over. Guard and Matilda were now Mr. and Mrs. Guard McCall.

Their laughter was shattered by a sudden cry from someone running across the clearing. "Mr. Robertson, Mr. Robertson. Come! Hurry! Oh, Mr. Robertson, someone has shot and kilt an Indian!"

Guard trembled. He put his new wife back into her parent's cabin and ran to get his new gun, the one that the Long Hunters had brought him. He hoped that he wouldn't need it, but he just might.

For the next few minutes everything was chaos. An Indian, Cherokee Billy, was dead. The men formed a posse and soon located a very scared, mentally deranged man. The man, William Crabtree, was from the Wolf Hill Settlement, and was afraid of all Indians. He had no other motive for the shooting.

The festivities ended abruptly. The Indians left in a frightened hurry. They felt betrayed. As a result, Col. Robertson soon left with another party for Chota to work at healing wounds caused by this infamous act.

The rest of the summer was as nearly normal as possible for Guard and Matilda. The fear of an Indian attack loomed over them. It was always there, this anxiety tucked into the back of their minds. They tried not to think of it, but threw themselves into their work. Work was never over because survival was always the uppermost in their minds; not just their survival from the Indians, but from want and from the elements. Gathering in fuel and food for the winter was a never-ending summertime job.

Guard had traded furs for a spinning wheel. He was now building a loom for Matilda. It would take up a lot of the floor space in the small cabin, but it was a necessary thing. He had planted a small patch of flax for her, and had arranged with another settler to obtain wool from his sheep.

He was also helping her make soap and candles. This was a job that was shared with her parents.

But the biggest chore for Guard at this time was to fell and gather hardwood logs to cut for a puncheon floor. The process was slow, and often he had to get help in doing this. It was something that was difficult for one man to do. He needed strong help. The men of the settlement were always eager to be of help to Guard, and he always repaid them with his help whenever it was needed. These men had a lot of skill and knowledge that he didn't have. Guard was very appreciative.

It was late summer when a circuit-riding preacher visited the Sycamore Shoals settlement. He was to stay there for two or three weeks before moving on to the next stop. He would be holding services mornings and evenings.

Guard and Matilda, along with most of the other settlers in the entire Watauga Assembly, attended the meetings. However, Guard left the first meeting very disturbed. He lay awake that night tossing and turning. After a while, he arose. He walked around outside of the cabin. Guard looked at the stars and tried to tell God about his fears. After a few minutes, he returned to his cabin, lit a candle, and got his Ma's Bible. He began reading in the Book of John. He read until he came to the third chapter and the sixteenth verse:

For God so loved the world, that he gave his only begotten Son, that whosoever believeth in him should not perish, but have everlasting life.

This verse didn't say that it was for just a few. It said, "Whosoever believeth..."so he read on. Soon he came to the fifth chapter and the twenty-fourth verse:

Verily, verily, I say unto you, He that heareth my word, and believeth on him that sent me, hath everlasting life, and shall not come into condemnation; but is passed from death unto life.

Guard read it again and again. Suddenly he understood.

He ran over to the bed and shook Matilda. "Here, listen, the Bible says, 'Whosoever,' Matilda. That's not what that preacher-man said. Matilda, he said that not everyone is chosen, not all are predestined, just the ones who are the elect. Oh, Matilda, whosoever means me. But how, what do I do? I don't know. I can't ask him. I just can't. But I will find out, I will...."

"Hush, Guard, you're talking like an Anabaptist. My grandpa always said that the Anabaptists were heretics. Please don't talk like this, don't, please don't." Matilda was pleading with him. Her eyes had taken on a look of fear.

He kissed her tenderly and said, "Don't worry, my love. Go back ta sleep. I'm talkin' with jest you. I've got to find answers before I say anything to anybody else. I've got to find answers and I will...."

But Guard stayed up long hours that night and many more nights. He had his spiritual appetite whetted, and he knew that he must find answers. One night while he was studying on this subject, he remembered where he had heard that word "Anabaptist" before. That's what they called that preacher-man who took his brother. He knew that, he had talked about it, but just now it became real to him. If he could just find Garse, then maybe he could find some answers.

These things were always in the back of Guard's mind, but many weeks were to pass before any answers would come.

The fear of an Indian uprising was more prominent that it had ever been since they had been there. Dragging Canoe, the Cherokee War Chief, had been stirring up trouble with the Indians in the entire Cherokee nation. He had been hostile ever since Cherokee Billy was killed. He had not wanted peace even in the beginning and had accused his father, Attakullakulla, who was the Cherokee Peace Chief, of being a soft old man. The settlers lived with this cloud of anxiety and dread over them.

Guard had the added worry of Matilda. She was with child. Her time would come in late summer. They were both very excited and happy. Matilda insisted that she was able to do any work that she'd always done, yet they always welcomed the help that her parents gave to them.

Even though Guard was forever busy, he always tried to take a few minutes before going to bed at night to read from his Ma's Bible. Sometimes anxiety about his soul weighed heavily upon him; other times he turned it off and went on to sleep. At times, though, he and Matilda would discuss what he had read, but he never brought up the subject of "Anabaptist" again. The wondering about it though was always there. What did it mean? What was so wrong about it?

Guard needed to go down to Brown's Trading Post on the Nolichucky River before the baby came. He would be gone about three days, four at the most. Matilda would stay with her parents until he returned. He gathered up all the things he had for trading and left out early on a Tuesday morning. He would surely be back home by Friday or Saturday.

Matilda insisted that he not go alone. Since the fear of an Indian uprising was constantly on their minds, he made arrangements with some other men to go with him. One of them knew the route, having been there many times before.

Guard was lighthearted as they left the Sycamore Shoals settlement. They had to travel a few miles back up the same trail they had taken from Carolina. Guard couldn't help wondering about what might have happened to Mr. Forrester, but that episode of his life seemed so long ago and so far away it was more like a bad dream.

They turned into a narrow gorge cut by a winding creek.

"Hain't too far up this here creek 'till we'll see some prize flat land," Josiah Bennett said. "Iron ore up here, too, may be that someday we can mine hit, and make good use of hit.

"Great possibilities, great possibilities. Well, jest lookie over there Indian campsites. Indians have hunting camps all over this area." He then pointed to a majestic mountain rising to the south of them. "That's the Un-a-kee. That's what the Indians call it, the Un-a-kee."

Guard stopped. He bent over and picked up an Indian arrowhead. Several arrowheads were in sight around them. "Let's jest hope they're all gone. I jest don't cater to beholdin' any of 'em right now."

As they walked on, the conversation went from one thing to another, and soon the subject of religion came up.

"You fellers foller the teaching of that circuit-riding preacher-man awhile back?" Guard asked the others, cautiously.

"Never did give it much thought," Josiah Bennett answered. "Guess I'm not one of the elect, least that's what my Ma thought, so I jest never did think they's much use fer me to try."

"Pshaw...Josiah, that's ridiculous," interrupted Ezekiel Collins. "Hain't no God of love works thata way. Used to think that a way myself till I heerd that Anabaptist preacher down in Caroline, down in Wake County. I know some people call 'em heretics, but they make powerful good sense to me."

Guard stopped dead in his tracks. "Anabaptist. What's Anabaptist?"

"Well," Ezekiel Collins answered. "They're called Baptists by some folk. Ana means against baptism."

"Goodness, then hit's no wonder they're heretics if they don't believe in baptism," spoke up Josiah Bennett.

"Didn't say that," interjected Ezekiel. "They're the baptizingest people I ever knowed of. They jest don't baptize their babies. Say they don't see no need of it. Say babes can't be lost 'til they grow some, and that makes a lot of sense to me.

"That hain't all they do that causes trouble. They're in conflict with Calvin about other things. They teach that whosoever will believe will be saved, and that makes sense to me too, none of that elect stuff."

The conversation then went to something else. But Guard's mind stayed on the remarks that he had just heard. Maybe he was about to find answers.

They neared a trail that followed a large creek that had headwaters on the Un-a-kee Mountain. Guard looked up at the mountain. It was enveloped in a hazy mist.

"That there mountain," said Josiah, "is covered with big grassy places, called balds. They attract deer, buffalo, and other grazing animals. They say that they cross there on their way to the salt pits up in Virginie."

They followed the creek until it reached the Nolichucky River. They remembered the warning given them about getting into the waters of the 'Chucky. Robertson had told them that it was dangerous and treacherous, having currents that were always changing, and it had suck-holes. He had told them that the word *Nolichucky* itself meant dangerous waters, and to just follow the river bend. It would take longer, but it was safer.

It was around noon on Wednesday that they arrived at the "Chucky Trading Post." Mr. Brown greeted them. He spoke to Ezekiel Collins and Josiah Bennett, both of whom he knew and then turned to Guard.

"Don't believe I know ye, young feller. Saw you up at Watauga, but don't recollect yer name."

"Sorry," Josiah said, "This here is McCall...Guard McCall. Come down from up around Wake County with Robertson."

Brown frowned, "McCall...you say...you the same boy what was bound out to that scoundrel Forrester? I heerd about ye. He was a regular tyrant."

Guard trembled, but he didn't answer.

"Don't be afeerd. Ole Forrester is dead, been quite a spell now. Anyhow, everybody knew that he used ya. Come on in and let's get a little tradin' done."

After they went in, an old man who had been seated on a barrel near the door, rose up and walked in. "McCall, did I heer ye say, McCall? Could it be that ye're Garse McCall?" he asked.

Guard turned ashen white, he grabbed the old man's arm. "Garse, ya know Garse? Garse is my brother. Where is he? Tell me!"

"Don't rightly know where he is. Ya sure do favor him. Brother, ya say? Jest know that Garse is one of them Anabaptist preacher fellers over in Caroline. Heh, ye're brothers ...Are ye' now?"

Guard was happy, sad, and puzzled all at one time. Happy because he had had some news about his brother. Sad because it seemed as if Garse had enemies. And puzzled about it all.

Mr. Brown went on talking, "Joe, here, is a trader. He carries supplies over the mountains. There's a gap just south of here that allows fer passage from Carolina. It follers the gorge cut by the Nolichucky River. Hit sure is dangerous, but

Ole Joe makes the trip three, four times a year."

Guard turned around to the old man that was called Joe. "When ya go back over the mountain and if ya get the opportunity, will ye get word to Garse that I'm alive, and that I would love to see him? Tell him that I'm married and soon to be a papa."

It rained on them almost all the way home. The rain combined with the muddy trails slowed their trip down considerably. Guard was quiet as he sloshed along in the rain. He scarcely felt the water as it ran off his face and hair. He was deep in memory...memories of childhood before Pa had died. Memories of the bad days with Mr. Forrester. He was also filled with plans for the future. Plans of trying to get to see his brother again.

Chapter Nine

Guard almost ran the last mile home to his cabin. He went as fast as he could go and lead the mule laden with materials and supplies. He was eager to see Matilda and tell her about Garse. As soon as he unloaded the supplies, he hurried over to the Long's cabin.

He was met by Mr. Long as he approached. "Guard, Son, glad ya got back. Tildie is in a bad way. Been laborin' all day. Hit's a hard birth, the granny-woman says. We'll jest have to wait and pray. Babes that come early sometimes cause trouble. Jest don't get yer hopes up too high, Son. The Almighty knows what is happening, but we still need to ask Him fer help. Let's go down by the river."

"But...how? Why? It's not time. Is she gonna be alright? I need to see her...let her know I'm back. I gotta go in there!"

"No, Son, we can't help none in there, but we can out here. Let's go."

Guard and his father-in-law walked down the path. The same path he and Matilda had walked the night he had proposed to her. Guard fell on the soft mossy carpet crying. "Please God, help my Matilda. Let her be alright. You say to call. I read it in the Book, and I'm calling. Please, Lord."

"Guard, Pa...It's over." Guard looked up. Her Ma was standing above them on the hill. "Come on," she smiled. "Matilda wants you. She is fine."

Guard jumped up running and shouting. "Thank you, God. Thank you, thank you." He stopped outside the cabin door, caught his breath, smoothed back his auburn hair, and opened the door.

Matilda was almost lost in the depth of the corn shuck bed tick. Her face was tired and white, but she was smiling. He tiptoed over to her side. "Oh, My Love, My Love. I'm sorry I was gone. Are ye alright?" His voice broke and he kissed her.

Until now, he had not thought of the baby. His mind was completely filled with his wife. Her golden hair encircled her head like a halo. She looked to him like an angel.

He looked up to see a neighboring woman who served as a mid-wife, a granny-woman, carrying a bundle toward him. From the blanket came a whiny sound. His hands trembled as he reached out. She laid the bundle in his arms. He turned to his wife.

"Your son," she said. "He's very small and fragile. We'll have to be careful with him."

"And with you too, My Love. Ye're very small, also. Now ye git some rest. Ya look pretty tired." His chest swelled with the pride of a new papa holding his firsborn. When the baby began to cry he returned his son to the granny-woman and left.

Once outside, Guard put his hands over his face and cried. His mother-in-law put her arms around him. She told him about the happenings of the last few hours.

Guard looked up. "Well, thank God. It's over. He needs a name. Josh, Joshua McCall, after my Pa. That's what we'll call him. How does that sound?"

Little Joshua grew by leaps and bounds. His size had nothing to do with his strength. He got along a lot better than his mother did. She was slow getting her strength back. Guard was so grateful for the help that her parents provided them, both in the harvesting and in the care of the little family.

One evening in late Indian summer, Guard finished up his work and came into the cabin. Mrs. Long was tending the baby while Matilda was stirring the stew over the fire in the yard. The smell of corn pone arose from the bake oven in the shed. A pot of hot sassafras tea, hung steeping on the tripod over the fire. Stewed, dried blackberries added their aroma to the already tantalizing smell of supper. Matilda smiled, her face was radiant. Her long golden hair was wound up in a bun at the base of her neck. Little moisture curls encircled her face.

"Oh, Guard, Ma heard that the preacher-man is at Fort Shelby and will be here in the next few days. We must see him and get baby Josh baptized," she said as she ladled the stew into the wooden trenches. She placed a small crock of honey and one of curdled cream on the table as she talked.

Guard didn't answer. Somehow he knew the time that he had been dreading had arrived. He knew that sooner or later he would have to face this. He remembered the distress of the ladies when they first arrived because an infant had died without baptism. He could not accept infant baptism for his son. He didn't know why, not yet he didn't, but he couldn't let this be done. This very concern led Guard to return to his Bible study that very night.

The next morning, Mr. Long came by to help Guard bring in some late squash to store for winter. "Won't be long 'till we'll dig these 'taters," he said. "'Low you've made a few, what with the mice and other varmints around. Ye've done right well...ever little bit helps. Corn looks good and with what meat ye've got put up, ye'll make it.

"Seed a bee tree up the hollar. Reckon we can rob it and have some sweetnin' and then we'll get the sorghum biled down. Hit didn't do too good, but there's a little." Then he added, "Ma says Josh will get his baptizin' as soon as the preacher rides in."

Guard stopped, cleared his throat, and gathered up courage. "No, reckon not. I jest ain't got my mind set clear on this thing yet. Don't zackly feel right 'bout it. Gotta think this thing through a while longer...'sides, I can't figger out the reason."

Mr. Long wiped his hand over his face. "You're a strange feller, Guard. All babies I ever knowed was baptized. Hit's jest always been...reckon that's reason 'nuff. Men that knows more 'bout the Word than I do says that it's 'post to be done. That's good 'nuff fer me. Now, that baby is my grandson, and it jest seems to be unchristian, that's all. Jest plain unchristian. But you're the pa, though. Can't argue with ye, but ye'd better think it over."

"Well, I've done thought it over, and I reckon I'll jest wait, least till I'm satisfied in my own mind that it ought to be done. Reckon I got plenty of time." Guard answered emphatically, then he added, "Nuff said."

Matilda was quiet that evening. Guard figured that the folks had already told her of his decision. After the evening meal was cleared away, she said, "My husband, I'll back you up in your decision, but we've got to face all the settlers. They say that Daniel Boone's wife will be stopping over at the Robertson's with her children, so's they can be baptized. These women don't understand, but I'll abide with ye."

"Thank ye, Matilda, I's hoping ye'd 'bide by my decision. I jest don't know. Last night I read where going to Heaven required that we be like little children, but it don't say they's baptized first. I jest can't figger out how a few drops of water poured on my son's head is gonna make him any better."

Chapter Ten

The entire Overmountain area was growing. In the three years since they'd been across the mountains, hundreds of settlers had arrived. They covered an area of fifty to sixty miles. Each time a stranger came by the Watauga Settlement, Guard would look carefully to see if maybe it was Garse. Why? He didn't know why, except that the desire to see his brother was so strong. It had become especially strong since that day in the Chucky Trading Post when he had heard that Garse was bound out to an Anabaptist preacher-man, and was also an Anabaptist preacher himself.

Since arriving west of the ridge in the Overmountain country, Guard had not been any farther away from his cabin on the banks of the Watauga River than the trading post at Chucky. Most of the other men had made a trip back into the Carolinas for supplies that couldn't be gotten as yet in their area. So at the last meeting of the men, he had volunteered to travel in the next group back over the Roan to the Carolina country. The decision was made largely from his desire to find his brother, and possibly find out answers to his deeper questions.

"What ya studyin' on?" Matilda asked him as she put her arms around him. "Ye're awfully quiet tonight."

"I'm studyin' 'bout goin' back over the mountains fer supplies. Figger hits 'bout time fer me to take a turn. We've not 'nuff supplies laid by to see you through till I git back. Your pa and ma be here. Don't cherish the thought of leavin' ye and Josh, but I feel that I'd better take my turn.

"We've not seen any Indians in a while, although we've heerd rumors that Draggin' Canoe is still trying to excite his braves, but he's been trying that ever since Cherokee Billy was shot. Ye'll jest have to take Josh and go to yer folks' cabin. Hit's closer to the fort."

"When ye leaving?" she asked softly.

"Don't know, maybe in a fortnight. Wanna go and git back 'fore the cold weather hits too strong. Hit gits cold on them high mountains. Ya remember, hit's a great deal more airish up high than down here."

He gathered her into his arms. "Matilda, I love ya so much. I'll sure be missin' ya, but there's jest some things a body's gotta do, and I gotta do this."

Guard spent the next few days getting things ready for the trip. He was anxious to be gone, yet he didn't want to leave Matilda and Josh. This desire to find his brother and so seek deeper answers was eating at him until he could scarcely think of anything else.

Guard rose before dawn on the morning of his departure. He looked down at the face of his lovely, sleeping wife. This life was hard on her. It held very little beauty, very little comfort, but she accepted it without complaint. He wanted her to have better someday. But right now, he was determined to bring back some nice things to surprise her. Maybe some kind of fancy dish, or some nice dress goods with all the trimmings. She deserved it. He wanted her to have something special.

Then he looked down at the sleeping boy and smiled. He would just have to bring something special for him, too.

First light would be here soon. His gear was already assembled. He'd pack the mules before long, but for now he'd just read his Ma's Bible.

Guard went out and sat on the stoop to catch the first rays of light. He opened the Bible and searched until he found, "...Whosoever shall call on the name of the Lord shall be saved."

"That's anyone," he thought, "and that's me."

"Oh, Lord, I'm being drawn on this trip. I don't want to leave my family, but I must. God, I don't even know effen ye hear me, but effen ye do, please take care of them. And God, I know that they's God-fearin' folk here. I know they is, God. I hain't sayin' they's not. But I jest can't rest easy. I want answers, answers that I can rest with. Lord, Ma always said to pray. The Longs say to pray. So, Lord, effen ye hear me, help me find my brother, and help me to find answers."

The door opened and Matilda came out. Her hair tumbled down around her shawl-covered shoulders. She shivered and moved closer to him. "Guard," she whispered, "be careful and hurry back. We'll miss you, Josh, me, and the new wee one that be here come spring."

In his surprise, tears came. "I can't leave you, not now. I remembered what happened the last time."

"Hush, My Love, you must go. Believe the Book. God can watch over you there and look over us here. We'll be fine. Believe that. Go with our love. Now get gone. The rest of the party will be awaiting for you."

The early morning sun formed an ethereal halo around her as he walked away. He kept looking back, feeling both happy and sad.

She waved good-bye.

The tired and dirty party of backwoodsmen arrived at the trading post and mercantile in North Carolina about a week later. First stop was at the mercantile to have their pelts weighed and recorded for the later purchasing of goods. Guard was grateful that the Overmountain settlements would soon have trading centers. That would offer these supplies now available only at these distances.

He laid his pack of furs on the floor, untied them, and spread them out. After bickering and bartering, Guard and the merchant arrived at a fair price. His amount was entered in the ledger and then the clerk asked for his name.

"McCall. Guard McCall."

"McCall, ya say? Kin to that preacher-man McCall down to Willow Branch? Don't guess ye are, you way over there and him over here. 'Sides folks say he's a heretic. He preaches stuff some folks say 'tain't true. Don't know about stuff like that myself—don't keep abreast of religion."

With that the subject changed. Guard was glad. He figured that whatever this belief was, it wasn't popular, but at least now he had an idea of where to look for Garse.

The other men checked their furs in, and turned to leave. They needed a place to eat and sleep. A few houses down the street a sign read "Room and Board." They entered.

After a bath and a hot meal the men laid down to rest. Guard spoke, breaking the silence. "Ezekiel, you know these here parts. How would I get to Willow Branch? I'd like to visit that McCall feller. Might be he's my brother. Ain't seen him in nigh to fifteen years. Might be him. Kinda-young to be a preacher-man, but could be."

Ezekiel gave him the directions, and Guard rose up to leave. "Don't want to put ye out none, and hold us up gittin' back, so I'll be gone. Be back as soon as I find out."

The tiredness that had overwhelmed Guard was suddenly gone. With an energetic step he set out to the southeast of town. The cool darkness was both comforting and refreshing. With this new burst of energy, he found himself almost running. Ezekiel had said it was about seven and one-half miles. If he hurried he would be there before daylight.

A few houses were scattered here and there along the banks of the river. The lamps were still lit in a few of them. He smiled to himself as he thought of his family...and another little one on the way. Maybe this one would be a golden-haired girl just like his Matilda.

Just at first light, Guard entered the settlement called Big Rock Creek. Nothing was stirring but dogs and roosters. Soon though, farmers would be moving about performing morning chores. So he just sat down on a tree stump and waited until he saw someone that he could ask for directions.

It wasn't long until he saw a farmer's wife walking down a path to a spring. She was carrying two oaken buckets. "Good Morning, Ma'm. I'd like to ask you a question." Afraid that he might frighten her, he spoke very carefully and softly.

She stopped rather suddenly, and he realized that he had indeed frightened her.

"Don't be scared, Ma'm, jest want some information. I am lookin' fer someone. I was told that I might find him in this town. I need to see a man named McCall."

She looked him squarely in the eye, and then sternly asked, "And just what for do you want to see Mr. McCall?"

Guard didn't know what to answer. He was afraid that he might say the wrong thing. After the things that he had already heard, he needed to be very careful. So he didn't answer.

The farmer's wife set down her water buckets, placed her hands on her hips, and said, "Well, you his friend or his foe?"

"I don't know which, Ma'm, 'cause I don't know Mr. McCall. Just need to ask him something. Please, Ma'm, do ye know where abouts he lives?"

"That be the case, I'll tell ye." She pointed to a willow thicket on a nearby hill. "See that hill yonder? There's a trail around below it. Go round the hill a ways, and ye'll see a cabin. That's his'n." She picked up her bucket and walked on.

Guard called back a "thank you" and hurried toward the willow thicket. In a short time he had reached a rather large cabin. It was very neat looking. Flowers were planted along both sides of the path. He stopped, looked it over, took a deep breath, and gathered up all his courage.

Just as he began to walk up to the door, it opened and a tall young man with fiery red hair stepped out. He stopped when he saw Guard. Guard also came to a sudden halt. Memories began to stir. It was Garse. It had to be. He moved a little closer up the path. As he approached the man, he held out his hand. "Garse, is it you? Is it really you? Don't you remember? I'm Guard, your brother."

Immediately the two brothers were crying and laughing and talking all at one time.

Garse took Guard inside the cabin. He was talking so fast and crying so hard that he could scarcely tell his wife who their guest was.

But soon, his wife, Mary Kate, was preparing breakfast for them. As they talked, Guard looked around the cabin. There were curtains on the real glass windows. Homemade rugs covered the puncheon floors. Colorful things were everywhere. He thought about Matilda and how delighted she would be with cabin furnishings like these. Maybe, someday ...soon.

While they ate, stories were shared about their lives since they were indentured or bound out. In the midst of the conversation Guard interrupted with, "Garse, what's a Anabaptist?"

"That's what I'm called, Brother. I teach and believe that it is wrong to baptize a person until he has been saved, and then only by putting him all the way under the water. I believe that a man is saved when he has asked the LORD into his heart to be his Savior, and I don't believe that the Holy Bible teaches that infants are to be baptized. We're not against baptism, just infant baptism."

Guard spoke quietly, "I believe that way, too. I didn't let my son be baptized when the circuit rider came by. Me and my Matilda, we've been ridiculed about it, but they's things I don't understand. Lot's of things. I've been astudyin' on Ma's Bible, but I jest don't understand so much of it." He began to cry. "Garse, I'm feered I'm not one of the elect, one of the chosen. I read and I pray, but I don't feel right. I don't know what to do. I read and hit says, 'whosoever' and that's me, and then I heer some folks say different. Tell me what to do."

Garse went to the table and got his own Bible. He opened it and read, "'If thou shalt believe in thine heart...thou shalt be saved.' Guard, it's not an easy road to take a religious view that is different from most others. The man who took me in was a believer in the Baptist way. He was a good, gracious, kind man. He loved me and taught me much. He led me to Jesus for salvation. And when we moved here we found a following of Baptist ways already here.

"I'd like for you to understand that when the Lord gave Jesus to the world, He was a free gift. Free to all, to whosoever will come.

"The people that you've settled in with are good people. They're followers of a man named John Calvin. Their belief is like his. They're honest and good people, but we just don't see things like they do. We believe that Jesus died for everyone, including you, Guard."

"Garse, I want to believe. I've tried to believe. I read the Bible. I try to pray. Help me."

The two brothers knelt and prayed. When they arose they were brothers twice: blood brothers by birth, and blood brothers by the new birth.

Garse walked back to Big Rock Creek with his newly found brother. He promised to come over the mountains before cold weather set in.

Matilda was busy in the cabin when she heard her small son calling, "Pa, Pa!" She ran after him and soon fell breathless into her husband's open arms.

"Oh, Matilda, I found him, I found Garse...Oh, My Love, I can't wait to tell you about it all."

Guard unpacked the supplies and then turned to his wife. "Close your eyes, and hold your arms out."

She closed her eyes tightly, and he placed into her outstretched arms a bolt of soft blue fabric and yards and yards of lace and ribbon. He had even purchased mother-of-pearl buttons.

"Ohh...Guard, it is lovely. Oh, it is lovely. Thank you. Oh, My Love, thank you." She laughed and cried and danced around the room.

"Wait...my wife, stop again and close your eyes." This time he placed into her arms a pair of soft leather shoes.

All the while Joshua was running happily through the cabin pulling a little wooden horse on wheels.

Matilda was like a little kitten the rest of the day. She followed her husband everywhere soaking in everything that he said about his brother and her newly found sister-in-law.

"Oh, Guard, I just cannot wait to meet Mary Kate. Just think, a sister. I've always wanted a sister. Tell me again about her house. Tell me about the real glass windows, curtains, rugs, and tell me about the flowers. Oh, Guard, I'm so excited."

Guard reached inside his coat and pulled out a packet. "I almost forgot," he said in his slow drawl. "Mary Kate sent these flower seeds to ye. She wrote on them what they are and when to plant 'em." He couldn't help but smile at his child-like wife, she was so excited over the slightest little gift. He realized that these flower seeds were precious to her, for they represented beauty in her life.

He finished his chores, grateful to have the opportunity to do them, because it was his own farm, his home. He would tell Matilda later about his newly found peace with God.

Chapter Eleven

It was late fall and Guard was busy garnering fish and meat to be smoked and stored for winter. On this particular evening he had walked down into a field to check a rabbit box. To his delight there was a rabbit trapped in it. He walked on toward his cabin thinking just how pleased his wife would be with fresh meat for supper. This was a young and tender rabbit, so it would not take long to cook.

As he neared the cabin from the east, he saw a man walking in from the west leading his horse. Guard stopped and watched as the man came nearer. "It can't be...it is! It is Garse!" He cried aloud, "Garse...here I am, over here, Garse."

Garse broke into a fast run still holding on to his horse. The brothers embraced, and walked together toward the cabin.

"Matilda, come out here. We've got company."

She came out the cabin door, wiping her hands on her apron. She smiled as she held out her hand. "Garse! It's Garse, isn't it? I'd know you anywhere. Guard has spoken so of you."

Guard was proudly beaming, "My wife, Matilda, and this here little tyke is my son, Joshua, named fer our Pa."

Guard skinned and cut up the rabbit. The two men cooked it in the iron spider over an open fire in the cabin yard. Matilda put potatoes in the bake oven on the fire. When the rabbit and potatoes were done, she set out a dish of cold fried mush. They drank cold milk from the spring house. Later, they ate stewed, dried blackberries sweetened with honey. They visited late into the night before finally going to bed.

Next morning while doing the chores together, Garse said, "Brother, there's been some people of my religious persuasion just recently cross over through the gorge of the Nolichucky and through its gaps to the land claimed by Jacob Brown. These call themselves General Baptists. Some folks call them 'Freewillers.' They believe like I do, that God provides the way and the means of salvation and man accepts freely or rejects according to man's own will. Would ye care to venture down to see these folks with me?" Garse asked this question of his brother very cautiously, watching him as he spoke.

"Well, I'll check with Matilda, what with the baby comin' and all, I hate to leave her. I'd sure like to go. We'll see."

In just a couple of days, Guard and Garse were riding along the Doe River to a trail leading south toward the Chucky Settlement. Ezekiel Collins was with them. He had chosen a different trail than before to reach their destination. Instead of heading north to go out another stream and come down a cove leading off Unaka Mountain, they had moved along Buffalo Creek. This creek was unusual in that it flowed north. It was a narrow creek cutting deep into the soft limestone. The land around it was mostly flat and travel was easy. They soon reached the same large creek that they would have if they had gone the other route. Only this way was much easier and quicker.

Ezekiel pointed out the area called Greasy Cove. From a distance they could see some of the apparatus the bear skinners used when they boiled down bear fat to carry to the trading posts.

"All this here is part of Brown's claim," Ezekiel said. "Hit's gettin' settled down now pretty thick like. Lots of these folks are from up in Caroline, but they's a few from Virginie. From here on down the river, we'll be seeing more and more homesteads."

A couple of hours passed and they reached a large bend in the river. Towering above it was a large rocky ledge jutting out over the river. They stood looking at it, awed by its majesty. Ezekiel told them of the superstitions of the Indians about this rock formation. The Indians claimed that there were two facing profiles in the rock, which they called devils. Hence, the Indians called it a term that translated, "The Devil's Looking Glass." The Indians also told of Indian lovers who weren't allowed to marry and who jumped from it to their death below.

As they walked on down the riverbank, Ezekiel said, "Guard, you 'member the last time we came down here? We had to walk all the way around this big bend, 'cause 'long here are some dangerous suckholes, and we were cautioned not to get in the water to cross it. Well, now, jest a little piece farther down past the suckholes, they's a pole raft fer us to use. They's one on each side of the river. We need to be lookin' fer 'em. Hit sure will take a considerable space and time offen our journey."

Just a few more minutes passed when Garse called out. "Here it is, just like they said. It will take us two or three trips, but we'll make it. But what happens when we leave the raft, both of them will be on the same side of the river?"

"Oh, never mind 'bout that. They's folk around here that will see to it that the raft gits t'other side," Ezekiel answered. "Folks always look to such things that 'commodate other folk."

Garse was the first to speak after they got safely to the other side. "I've never seen such rich, flat bottom land. There's so much grassy land, man doesn't even need to clear a field for planting or for pasture. I've seen sheep, goats, and many cabins. No wonder so many people are arriving here to settle. Just wonder if any preacher ever comes by here to preach?"

Ezekiel answered, "Most of these here folks are Scottish descent, and they's mostly Calvinist. Heerd tell, though, some Anabaptists are over near the Beams, on the Watauga. Don't know, jest heerd hit."

Garse replied, "It is a shame. These folk need a preacher. They need the Word of God. Whenever we get down to the lower end of the Chucky Settlements, it may be we'll get some answers."

It was late afternoon when they reached a trading post farther down the river. The river along here was treacherous, and they didn't want to be traveling after dark in unfamiliar surroundings. Besides the clouds were low and dark with a strong wind blowing. It was getting colder. Snow flurries were likely. It was early yet for snow, but possible in mountainous areas. They entered the trading post which also served as an inn and a tavern. A large group of men were there.

One of the older men was speaking, "Yep, Jonesborough's getting to be a regular size town—soon we'll see a charter there. Never seen any place grow so fast. Good thing them Indians had all their problems. Sure has saved us a lot of 'em." The buckskin-clad man spat into the open fire and continued, "Hain't that what you say, Lt. Sevier?"

A handsome, medium built man spoke up. From his talk, it was obvious that he was well educated. "Yes, but let's not rest too assured. We know that Dragging Canoe is still trying to stir up the braves. We know that they have attacked in other places. I hear that they're planning an attack on our forts, and it may be soon. Because of this we had better get busy on finishing Fort Lee. It is just too far to get to safety at Fort Watauga or at Chucky. It's way too far."

Garse and Guard looked at each other and then at Ezekiel Collins. Their thoughts were of the settlers at Fort Watauga. Garse spoke quietly to his brother, "We have put our faith in the Lord. We are not to worry. We will finish our mission here and hurry back."

The next morning as they prepared to leave, they were pulled aside by the trader. "You men, be on the look out fer Injuns. Got a feeling that they're snooping around. Keep that rifle handy," he admonished.

They nodded and set out for the area at the base of a very large mountain. The trader told them to just follow the river, and they would reach the settlement they were looking for. They would recognize it because a waterwheel and grist mill were under construction. "Just stop and inquire there," he told them.

It was close to noon when they discovered the waterwheel. No one was around, that they could see, so they sat down to rest and wait. When they got quiet, they heard voices. They were too far away to distinguish what was being said. Quietly they moved in closer to the voices. It was men in prayer. Garse reverently bowed his head. Guard looked about him in wonder. It was unlike anything that he had ever heard.

"Oh, Lord, your children have ventured out by faith into this new land. We came because we felt direct guidance from You. We haven't asked for a life of ease, but for one of peace with Thee. Lord God Almightly, we need guidance. We need to know Your Word, Your ways. We've got the Book, but we need a preacher. Lord, you sent us here to be among those who have beliefs like ours. But we are ignorant of your Word. Use us...Send us a preacher, a leader. In Jesus' name. Amen."

Tears were flowing down Garse's sunburned cheeks. He looked at Guard with wonder. He spoke in an almost whisper, "I am the man. I am their preacher. God sent me."

The men from the settlement sat up most of the night with the travelers from Fort Watauga. They told a story of how they had banded together because of their religious beliefs. They had experienced persecution from the Particular Baptists, as well as from the English officials, and even from other groups. But in the midst of all this persecution, a great revival had swept through the mountain towns east of the ridges in North Carolina. This revival was a result of and the answer to, prayers of their little group of Anabaptists called Freewillers.

Guard didn't say anything; he just listened. He learned from their talk that Baptists in North Carolina were divided into two groups: the General Baptists and the Particular Baptists. The Particular Baptists were also against infant baptism, but still clung to a lot of Calvinistic beliefs, beliefs that a large number of the Baptists could not accept. These were called General Baptists. Some people called them Freewillers, for they felt that a man's salvation was between him and God, and his confession of faith in Jesus Christ. It was an act of a man's own free will to accept Jesus.

An elderly man spoke softly and with a tearful, broken voice, "Seems as if each time we begin to grow we have trouble. The Calvinistic Baptists would move into our area, and they would either build a church nearby and persuade our people to leave, or else some of 'em would join our group to cause confusion. It just seemed like trouble every way we turned. So we decided to come as a group and settle here. We came without a pastor. We've prayed ever since for leadership. If God sent us here, and we believe that He did, then He will send us a preacher."

Everyone sat silent for awhile. There was still a lot of questions in Guard's mind, but he did not interrupt the silence. Then an old man with a long white beard spoke up. "I'm old. I'm not a goin' to be here much longer, but I want to live to see our children educated in the Word, and walkin' in God's ways as we see them. We need a preacher who can teach our children to read, so they can study and know God's Word."

After a few silent moments, Garse solemnly spoke, "There's been an unexplained chain of events in my life. I was indentured to a kind Anabaptist preacher. He led me to the Lord, and another miraculous series of events have led me here. And I've been schooled, first by my Ma, then by the preacherman. Men, God sent me here. I am your preacher, but I'll have to go back to North Carolina and get my wife."

Tears of rejoicing began to flow freely from the men in this settlement. After prayers of thanksgiving to God, one of them asked a question, "Reckon what your wife will say? Will she want to come?"

"Oh, yes, she will come gladly. She loves the Lord, and she can also teach your children. She goes where I go. She has also suffered ridicule and longs for peace and freedom."

More plans were made, and more prayer was offered to God. The next morning they held a service for all the people. The women packed some food for them to take on their way. Garse assured them that he would do his best to return before bad weather. He also told them he thought that he had better come back down Roan Mountain, because the Nolichucky gorge was unfamiliar to him.

On the return trip up the Nolichucky, Garse was filled with rejoicing. He was making plans out loud. Guard expressed his joy that his brother would be near him. Other than that Guard said very little, but he was thinking. "What am I thinkin' 'bout? I believe like Garse. I did before I even knew about Garse's life. I've prayed for guidance. I can move with him. But I just wonder what Matilda will say? She doesn't share my beliefs, not yet. She doesn't understand yet, but she will."

There wasn't any time to discuss things with Matilda. He told her about his trip and about Garse's decision, but not about his convictions and his desire. Survival was taking on a new trend, Indians! An Indian attack was constantly a threat. This was an Indian strategy to unnerve them. It was designed to cause them to let down their guard and then an attack would come.

John Sevier, known by the people as Nolichucky Jack, was in and out of the settlement. Sevier and his family were well respected in all the settlement. He was also respected for his military knowledge and leadership. He, Captain Robertson, and other leaders were in very serious moods and were pushing for the men to help with the building of other forts for protection and for places to store supplies.

News came in with almost every visitor of an attack on some outlying group of cabins. The suspense was ever present, but no attack came here, not yet anyway.

Guard gave his required time helping with the general chores of the fort and of the settlement. Besides that, he had much to do in gathering in the winter's wood and other staples for his own family and for Matilda's parents. Mr. Long wasn't as strong as he was when he first came. The hard life in a short time had certainly taken a toll on him. Guard felt it necessary to help him all that he could.

In the back of his mind there was always a nagging worry about Matilda and the coming baby. Joshua had come early and with so much difficulty. He was afraid to leave her alone, and felt that he needed to be with her more.

When the work was finally caught up, Guard was more relaxed. He enjoyed the long evenings in the cabin with his family.

Guard watched Matilda lovingly as she tended to her chores of cooking, spinning, and caring for their son. "You're feelin' a lot better this time, ain't you, My Love? I watch you, and ya know it could be 'cause I am prayin' fer ya. Before I didn't have the comfort of real prayin' fer ya. Prayer has become so important fer me. Matilda, that's my burning desire—jest to pray and to study God's Word. I ain't got much education, but I am so thankful that I can read the Word. Jest wanted ye to know that I am prayin' fer ya and fer the wee one to come. I really do git assurance from my Bible. Assurance that God cares for us."

She smiled, "Why, Guard, that's the first time I've heard you call the Bible, 'My Bible.' You've always said, 'Ma's Bible.'"

"Wasn't aware of it, but I guess it is true. 'Tis mine, now. Well, it always was ever since Ma gave it to me, but now it's mine personal like. It is mine." He spoke in his slow, quiet voice.

Guard looked at her for a moment, then he spoke softly. "Matilda, I don't 'zackly 'terpet the Word like these folk here. These people are Calvinists...good people, but I just don't see eye to eye with them. Remember how they acted when we didn't baptize Joshua? Well, Wife, it will all be to do over when this wee one gets here. I don't want no trouble, but I want to worship God my way. My Love, I gotta ask you something, but don't want no answer yet. You know all about where Garse has gone. You know that settlement down on the Nolichucky? They's a whole community of folk there that see things jest like I do...call themselves Freewillers. They came down here from North Carolina jest 'cause of their troubles about their beliefs. They've got big dreams, Matilda, and they're a prayin' people. They want to educate their young 'uns. It hain't just 'cause Garse's gone down there to be their preacher. I will admit that Garse being there does help, but these are people like us. And our young 'uns will learn, really learn, not be like me. All I can do is read some, and do a little ciphering. They'll have a chance, a real chance."

Before he could say more, Matilda spoke to him, almost in a whisper. "You want to move down to the Chucky Settlements, don't you?"

"Yes, My Love," he looked at her tenderly. She was a true gift from God. Not yet twenty and yet so understanding of his feelings. He didn't want to hurt her or for her to be unhappy, so he said, "Now, don't ya answer yet. Jest think on it, and directly you can tell me. We wouldn't go until spring after the baby comes. When Garse came through several weeks ago with Katie, he said if we would send him word he would have things ready for us. Matilda, those are the kindest folks I've ever seen. They've got so much love. They'd help us get settled. Maybe, just maybe, your folks will come too, that is effen we go."

He took down "his Bible" as had been his custom lately and read to them. His voice faltered because he wasn't a fluent reader. "If any man would be my disciple, let him deny himself and take up his cross and follow me," he read.

After praying for guidance, Guard sat for a long time with his open Bible in his lap, a smile on his face, and tears of joy in his eyes. He smiled at his lovely wife and went to bed.

Several times, Matilda tried to say something, but he wouldn't let her. Soon she was asleep. But Guard lay awake for a long time. He drew mental plans for a large cabin, one with two rooms connected by a smaller room. He'd have a fireplace in both rooms, and he'd have real glass windows and a good floor. He'd see that Matilda had real curtains on the windows. Every comfort he could manage he would see that she had it. Being with those God-fearing women would be so good for her. Their houses were closer together, and she would have neighbors. Water would be no problem; good springs were abundant...the plans began to fade. Guard fell asleep.

The next morning he awoke early. The smell of fried mush and molasses filled his nostrils. Chicory coffee smelled sharp and good. A crock of milk graced the table. Matilda had gotten up even before he had. He was surprised. Josh was pulling at him, "Git up, Pa, git up and eat."

Guard raised up on his elbow and looked at his wife. He felt that he was dreaming. Such a short time ago he had had nothing. Now, he had all this. It didn't seem real that Matilda was his wife, and this was his family. God was certainly good to him.

She smiled at him, "Get up and eat, Pa. We need to get fattened up if we're going to make a long journey come spring."

He just couldn't believe it. He got up, embraced her, and brushed tears from his eyes. "Oh, My Love, you sure ye'll be happy?"

"Yes, Husband, I go where you go. Now, eat up."

They agreed not to discuss this with the others, not even her Ma and Pa, not yet. They would write a letter to Garse and send it down to the Chucky Settlement with the next person who was going that way. Guard had heard that Lt. Sevier would be at Sycamore Shoals soon. Perhaps he would carry the letter down as he returned. At any rate, it wouldn't be very long until Garse would receive it.

During the next few weeks they studied the Bible and discussed salvation. They searched the Bible for answers to all their questions.

One evening, Matilda looked up tearfully, "Guard, I'm not saved. I'm not a Christian. Ma and Pa taught me about God, and what was right and wrong. I was baptized as a baby, but, Guard, I am not saved, not like the Book says, not like you are. Help me."

Together they knelt and prayed. Simply and sincerely Matilda McCall asked the Lord Jesus to come into her heart.

Being closed in during winter months more so than at any other time was a time of spiritual growth. They spent every available moment studying and praying.

Each Sunday, during the winter whenever the weather permitted, Guard, Matilda, and Joshua would walk over to her Ma's and Pa's cabin. Guard would take his Bible and would lead them in Bible study. Soon others began to attend. Guard was very careful not to mention any of the doctrines wherein he differed with them. He just did not know enough to discuss it, and then, too, he didn't want any arguments, least not until he knew more about the Word.

One Sunday morning, however, a woman spoke up, "Guard, you'd better see to it that you get your babies baptized when this 'un gits here. Can't take no chances."

Matilda turned ashen white. Guard looked up, "No Ma'm, can't take no chances, don't need to. My babies'll get baptized. That is, whenever they get old enough to make their own decision. We'll jest have to wait 'til they're old enough to decide."

A man spoke up, "You sound like one of them Anabaptist

people called Freewillers. We's plagued with 'em in Caroline."

Guard smiled, "Well, come to think of it. I guess that's jest what you might call me, a Freewiller."

After this, the people who had been attending the Bible study stopped. They offered no explanation. But Guard knew. The feelings of disapproval and rejection were present each time Guard or Matilda went out among the other settlers. It was hard for them to believe that people could change and be so intolerable of those who differed in their religious beliefs.

"Don't worry, My Love, we'll soon be gone. Things will be different down on the Chucky River," he reassured her.

Mary Kate was born in late March. She was lovely. Her hair was a mixture of her mother's golden blonde and her father's auburn locks. It looked like the golden edge on the leaves of his Bible. Matilda had such an easy time in this delivery. Her Ma was all the help that she needed. Guard said that this was an answer to his prayers.

It wasn't long until Matilda was on her feet helping to get things ready to move. A few days before they were to leave, her Pa and Ma came over to visit. Her father said, "Well, children, our hearts are broken that yer leavin' and takin' our precious grandbabies. I'm gonna travel with ya, me and Ezekiel, to help out, and effen I like what I see, I'll jest come back and git Ma. We just can't stand to be so far away from our wee ones."

Then to Guard he said, "Don't blame ya, son. A man's gotta do what a man's gotta do. I did when I left Carolina."

Chapter Twelve

It took them over a week to reach the settlement of the lower Chucky area. They traveled slowly in order not to tire out the new mother and the small children. When they arrived they found that Garse had made arrangements for them to have temporary shelter until a permanent home was built.

Mr. Long was helping with the routine chores that pertained to their stay. He commented on the warmth and friendliness of the people. "Children," he said, "I like it here. Me and Zeke'll go get your ma. We'll be back as soon as we can. Think Zeke'll move down her, too."

Soon the men were making plans for a large cabin for all of them. Mr. and Mrs. Long, Guard, Matilda, and the children would all live in one large cabin. They felt that the women and children would be safer when the men had to be gone, and that if they lived together they could share in the chores.

They found a nice place near a small creek. There was a ledge which protruded from behind the house site which would be a natural root cellar. A small spring bubbled up on one side of the cavern and ran down to the creek just a few yards away. This would be ideal for a spring house. While checking it for snakes or other animals, Guard and Mr. Long noticed that a small open-ended chamber extended to near the cabin site.

"I believe we could use this as an escape from the Indians if we so needed," Guard said to his father-in-law. "We could have an openin' behind the woodbox at the fireplace and hide it with a log and dirt enclosure. Believe we could fix it so no one would guess. Then I'd feel a lot better 'bout them effen we were out away from the cabin."

Soon they were all working very hard at raising a cabin.

All the men of the community helped. It was back-breaking work felling logs of nearly the same size, rolling them down to the site, notching them, and then raising them to make the walls.

While the men worked on the building, the women cooked for the work crews. It took nearly three days to raise the double cabin with an attic, and to roof and floor it. They left openings for the windows. Guard made shutters and placed them over the openings, with the promise of real glass windows very soon. He even sent word by a neighbor to the trading post to place an order for the window panes. They would be in in about four months if they were lucky.

Matilda and Katie became very close. They felt like real blood sisters. Katie was quick to confide in Matilda of her desire for a baby. Because she had none, she became like a second mother to Joshua and Mary Kate, her namesake.

The apple trees that had grown up from the seed carried over the mountains and planted along the Watauga River had been carried to the Chucky settlement. Guard had been very tender with them, and he carefully transplanted and watered them. Soon they, too, were flourishing.

He had been able to trade around and had acquired seeds for other vegetables and grains. When their cow came fresh, they traded one of her twin heifers for a couple of lambs. A neighbor had given them a laying hen. Soon they had the beginnings of all they needed in their new home.

The neighbors were very considerate in helping with things like stuffing bed ticks, gathering river rocks of uniform size for the fireplaces and like chores. They had even helped them to build an outdoor oven. This was an extra blessing in the hot summertime.

The women of the settlement showed Matilda and her mother where the vat was they used for making lye for soap and for fixing hominy. These things were often a community project, they were told.

In the fall, after all the necessary building was completed and just before the crops were ready for the main harvest, Guard and Matilda received word that their window panes were at the trading post. So they took the nicest of their trading pelts left from the past winter, and mounted their horse to travel to the post. It was about twenty miles from their cabin, so they left early one morning in order to return before dark.

Matilda was chatting happily as they rode along. She was so excited about having curtains and colorful trimmings for her home. She talked of dying the yarn into bright, beautiful colors for weaving. She talked of braiding and weaving rugs and coverlets.

Her arms were wrapped tightly round her husband's waist. He felt her body stiffen and tremble as they approached the trading post. She was frightened at the sight of a large group of Indian ponies tethered outside the trading post.

Her husband squeezed her hand and said, "They're generally here most any time. They trade here, too, you must remember. They're probably some of the same braves you've seen at Sycamore Shoals. Now, effen they hain't, ye'll be a strange sight to them, jest as they are to ya. Jest don't ya show no fear...don't be afeerd none. They might even touch your golden hair. Some of them have never seen beauty like yours. Jest remember, I am here."

Once inside, Matilda stayed close to her young husband. He led her to a counter with bolts of calico and muslin. She tried not to show her fear, and was turning to carry a bolt of muslin to the trader when she stopped suddenly.

Coming toward her was the most striking Indian squaw she had ever seen. Her dress of white buckskin was almost to her ankles. Her beaded moccasins were also white. Her long, blue-black braids were entwined with ropes of colorful beads, and on her arm were the wings of a white bird, a swan, she was to find out later. Her eyes were bright and she was intelligent looking. Walking with an air of dignity and authority, she stopped and looked right at Matilda and smiled. Without a word she left, followed by many half-naked braves. Matilda stood there in wonder, watching the entourage as it left. She was awe-stricken and speechless. Then she realized that the others were just as motionless as she was. While they watched, the Indians mounted their ponies and followed the squaw down the trail.

A man they recognized as John Sevier came from the back room. He watched with them before he spoke. "There is a great lady," he said. "She is our friend. Her name is Nan-ye-hi, or as we say, 'Nancy.' She holds the position of 'Beloved Woman' among the Cherokee. She acts as a voice of authority in the decision-making of the tribal council. Nancy is peace-loving. She wants us and her people to get along and learn from each other. But she tells me that the War Chief, Dragging Canoe, who is her cousin, is trying to stir up a bunch of renegade Indians. Men, we need to be on the alert for surprise attacks and ambushes. She just promised me that if she can't control the council she'll do her best to warn us if they do decide to attack."

Matilda listened as the men discussed the problem. Some of them called the Indians "Red Savages." One man said that none of them could be trusted, and that the only good Indians were dead ones. The conversation was like a ball tossing between the men in the trading post and Mr. Sevier as to the merits of the Indians.

After the commotion died down, they purchased their muslin and a few staples. The glass windows were carefully packed to keep them from breaking and put into the large saddle bags for safety. They were even able to get some real tea. This would really please her ma and pa. They often lamented the fact of no real imported tea in the wilderness.

They mounted the horse and began the ride back in the direction from which they had come. Matilda didn't say anything for awhile. But she fearfully thought that she saw an Indian behind every tree.

After awhile, she spoke, "Guard, does God love Indians too? Do they have souls? Can they go to Heaven?"

He slowed the pace of the horse. "Yes, I reckon so. The Book says that God so loved the world, and I reckon that Indians are part of the world. Sure, they've got souls, and effen they accept Jesus as their Savior they'll go to Heaven."

"Guard," she whispered, "do you reckon anybody ever tells them Indians about Jesus?" She was almost in tears.

"Don't know, My Love, but effen we ever git an opportunity to tell an Indian about Jesus, we will, but now we'd better move along, or we won't git back by dark."

Chapter Thirteen

Guard was so busy the next few weeks and everything was so peaceful that Indians were almost forgotten. White muslin curtains hung on the real glass windows. The food supply in the root cellar was increasing. The babies were growing. And the church was almost finished.

The men were putting the finishing touches on the mud plaster that was to serve until boards could be cut and planed for the inside walls. Even Ezekiel Collins was helping.

Guard spoke to his brother, "Hit don't look much like a church. But I reckon we're the real church, and I reckon we're all lookin' forward to the meetin' comin' up soon's it's done."

His preacher-brother answered, "The Lord is certainly blessing us, that's for sure. Katie'll be having our baby soon. You know, we never thought we'd ever have one. I, too, am looking forward to the meeting. Been praying about it. Got some good books given to me. Several folks around here had books, books that a preacher needs. Now, I got a lot to study on.

"Mrs. Coggins, she's got a lap organ and says that she'll play it for services. Yes, Brother, I am getting pretty fired up. These Sunday afternoon services on the hillside for our people are good, but I do believe we'll have people come from miles around who are hungry for the Word. That's why I'm grateful that the harvest is almost over."

Meeting time came. Services were scheduled for morning and evening each day. The services were to begin on Sunday. On Sunday morning the crowds gathered early. There was rejoicing among the older people just because they finally had a building for God's glory. Tears were shed and neighbors met and greeted each other with rejoicing and shouting. Their rejoicing was interrupted by a man from farther down the river. He was riding with such a rapid speed that his horse was in a foamy sweat. The rider and the horse were both out of breath.

"Indians, renegade Indians, they're burnin' and scalpin' everywhere along the way. Git ready and good luck." He turned to ride off, when one of the men stopped him and gave him a fresh horse on which to continue his journey.

Garse called the people to order. "Now folks, if you all agree, we will have a prayer service and prepare to defend ourselves. Some of you live too far away to make it back home. We're better able to defend ourselves as a group than if we were scattered around for miles. For this we can be thankful. Let's have prayer."

They knelt and began to pour their hearts out before God. They prayed for protection and for courage. They prayed until their voices arose in a mighty crescendo, and the sound echoed throughout the hills outside the crude log church building.

The sound reached the ears of a band of crouching, painted Cherokees who were ready to strike. They understood that this sound had something to do with the settler's ritual to their God. Being superstitious, the Indians waited. The thundering rumble of prayers began to subside, and the Indian warriors prepared again to strike.

But then, suddenly from inside the church came a terrible sound, a sound that the Indians did not recognize. They thought this was the voice of the white man's God answering them. For inside the little church, which was like an echo chamber, the praying people had arisen from their knees and began to sing a song of praise. Mrs. Coggins had begun to play on the lap organ. The sounds emitted from this instrument were indeed not very melodious. They were loud and together with the troubled, yet happy songs that the group of Freewillers were singing, the Indians were set to fear. The white man's God was answering them, and the Indians were afraid.

The Cherokee braves regrouped to evaluate the situation. They decided that perhaps the white man's God would go to sleep when night came, and they would just wait until darkness fell.

The Christians spent the afternoon resting and praying. The children gathered with Katie and Matilda and practiced their reading skills using the Bible as their textbook. The ones who had traveled the farthest distances from home had brought food, so they shared it with the others and none left the church.

In the southern Appalachian Mountains night comes on slowly. Twilight shadows skip and play among the trees and creep up in waves over the hills and vales. Each cove takes on a separate identity before darkness finally settles in. In some areas deep in ravines or hollows the darkness is very deep, except on nights when the moon is at its fullest. This was one of those dark nights with no moon.

The Cherokee chieftain decided that surely in darkness like this night the white man's God would sleep, and the victory would be theirs. They began to crawl back to the laurel thicket behind the church.

But, suddenly, the white man's God began to "scream" again. The people began singing in a rhythm with the "screams" of the organ which the Indians thought to be a god.

The petrified braves began to run! This God was not asleep. He did not sleep! He was awake by night and by day! They would have to come back when the white men were not in the house of their God.

The settlers in the little Free Will Baptist church stayed long and late that night. Garse preached his first sermon in the new building. When it was over, the ones who lived the nearest took the others to their homes. They were to stay until safety was more assured.

Early the next morning they agreed to continue with the morning service. Meeting had been planned and they would have it. Usually the worshipers would return home at night and come back the next morning after the morning chores were done. They would have two services and return home for evening chores, but this day they voted to go on without going home for chores.

Guard and his family were walking back toward the

church with the worshipers who had slept at their cabin. As they walked by the laurel thicket, Guard stopped. He motioned for the others to be quiet and cautious. He beckoned for Mr. Long to follow and they quietly slipped into the thicket.

No one moved nor spoke. The children were especially still. The events of yesterday had been so awesome that even the children sensed the urgency. A few minutes later, the two men came out of the laurel thicket carrying the limp, delirious, bronze form of a young, painted Cherokee brave.

Matilda gasped, "He's only a child! Is he alive?"

Guard nodded his head. "Yes, but I don't know...."

Mrs. Long looked at his head, "He's got a pump-knot on his head big as a goose egg. I figger he's been hit or he's run into something that has knocked him out."

"I figger that's what happened," her husband said. "He was just under a big low swung branch. He's hurt, that's fer sure. Figger he's got a broke foot 'er something. Can't figger out why the others left him. They don't generally do that."

Matilda turned white. "Guard, do you reckon this is our oportunity to tell an Indian about Jesus?"

They carried him back to the cabin and fixed him a pallet on the floor. Guard was afraid to leave the Indian lad. He knew that if he came to his senses, he would be wild and resist with force. He also knew that if he didn't come to his senses it might take a man to hold him down, and then there was always the possibility that the other braves would return looking for him. So he sent one of the men to tell the rest of the congregation that he was staying at home. He also requested prayer.

If the other braves returned, they came in and left very quietly without the settlers knowing it.

Some outlying cabins had been burned. Some cattle and other farm animals had been slaughtered while other animals were either driven away or escaped into the forest.

One family found their daughter scalped. She survived the ordeal through care and prayer, she had to wear a bonnet the rest of her life.

The meeting was postponed until the men could rebuild the destroyed cabins. Provisions were collected from all of the believers and distributed among those in need. The news of all the happenings traveled to other settletments, and when the services resumed there were many people riding in to hear the young preacher, Garse McCall. Some of these came for only the day services, others for the evening services, and a smaller number stayed for both. The meeting continued for two weeks. It was a time of great rejoicing as many souls were saved.

Other groups of believers joined in their services. One of these men came to visit Garse one day. "Brother McCall," he asked, "tell me how you can declare a man or a woman as 'saved' like you do. You don't put through no catechism or no questioning before the elders or anything like that."

"Well, Brother Taylor, I don't declare him saved. If he confesses that he believes in his heart, then the Word of God declares him saved. Brother, we're not taking anything away from you, but we believe that the Bible teaches that salvation comes on profession of faith."

The man continued, "You all are not the same as the New Lighters, or the Campbellites, are ye?"

"No, not the same. We believe in a man's free will being exercised. That's why some folk call us 'Freewillers.' A man can choose...but...in opposition to the New Lighters or Campbellites as you call 'em, we believe salvation comes before baptism, not auring it."

The visiting questioner continued his inquiries, "I don't mean to put you all down none. I like what I see. I feel good when I'm here, but there's still a lot of unanswered questions."

"Like what?" the young pastor asked.

"Well, for instance, like some of your practices, especially the one called 'foot washing.' Just never seen that done before, and I just don't understand it," spoke the puzzled questioner.

"We believe that our Lord commands us to do this, just like He did. He washed His disciples' feet, and said that we ought to do this too. We add this to our communion service, which by the way, is open to all believers, not just our members."

Mr. Taylor scratched his bearded chin. "I like what you

said the other night about, 'Gittin' right, livin' right, and then dyin' right.' Don't hear that often."

Garse spoke deliberately and slowly as he answered, "That doctrine has cost us a lot of persecution. People just don't understand us on this. We trace this part of our history back to a Dutchman named Jacob Arminius, who was in direct opposition to Calvin. He taught Free Will, Free Grace, and Free Salvation. This is the basis of our belief."

Mr. Taylor rose to leave. He still wore a puzzled expression on his face. Garse rose with him. "Come Sunday, we're having a baptism down at the creek there. You're welcome to join us. Come back to tonight's service if you can."

That night, some of the other men stayed with the Indian brave to relieve Guard so he could attend the meeting. He was glad because Garse called for all who were saved and not yet baptized by immersion to present themselves as candidates for baptism. At the same time, all who wished could come forward for membership in the Liberty Hill Free Will Baptist Church. Several came forward to present themselves for baptism and for church membership. As Guard stood watching, down the aisle came Matilda's parents. Their coming brought rejoicing and tears. Guard waited, then moved out. He had never been baptized, so this was his moment. On this night, Guard McCall and all of his family became part of the newly formed Liberty Hill Free Will Baptist Church.

Chapter Fourteen

The men had taken turns sitting with the injured Indian boy. The brave had come to, but it was hard for them to tell just what condition he was in. He acted frightened when they tried to talk with him. The only time he warmed up was to Joshua and Mary Kate, although their parents tried to keep them at a safe distance.

The brave watched suspiciously when they read the Bible. Each night when the family gathered for prayer and hymn singing he would act panic stricken. This was a source of worry to Guard. He prayed about it, and looked for every opportunity to try to communicate with him about Jesus.

Soon, Guard realized that the lad would respond to the word, "Indian." He used this to try to tell him about Jesus. He would point to the sky, then to the Bible, and to his heart, and say, "Jesus." Then he would point to the Indian boy and say, "Indian." Guard would smile, wrap his arms around the boy, and say, "Jesus loves Indian." Gradually the boy began to smile.

A few weeks after the organizational meeting of the little church, Garse brought his wife, Katie, to stay with Matilda and her family. He and Guard went a couple of miles back into the woods to rob a bee tree for honey. Mr. Long was left to stay with the Indian boy. Garse and Guard were successful in gathering a large supply of honeycomb and honey, and began the return trip home.

As they neared the settlement, Garse stopped and spoke in a scared whisper, "Smoke...Indians. They came back!"

The two frightened men abondoned the honey. Quickly and quietly as possible they hurried to the settlement. Four cabins were built close to the school/church building. The other cabins were all farther away from the church.

They stopped before they got to the edge of the wooded area. The church was not ablaze, but the four cabins were. Forgetting about the possibility of more Indians, they broke into a run. They cautiously approached the cabins. They thought Indians might be in the church or hidden in the brush around there, but they weren't.

Garse called, "Katie, Katie." His voice broke, his shoulders shook. He fell on the ground. "Oh, Lord, give me strength to accept this. Oh, Katie, Katie!"

Guard ran down behind the burning cabin. In one leap he was in the creek. He waded up to the dry ground and toward the ledge. Crawling and crying he pushed back the dense growth and there...huddled in the corner of the little cavern were the occupants of the cabin...and the Indian boy.

"Garse, Garse, they're here. They're alive. Oh, Hallelujah!"

And they were. Katie, Matilda and her babies, her parents, and the Indian lad.

The first one to speak was the Indian boy, "Jesus loves you," he said very slowly and deliberately, "Jesus loves Indian."

Matilda wept, "Guard, he saved our lives. We were all in the house. The boy sat up, looked frightened, and said, "Indians, Indians." We looked out and saw Garse's cabin ablaze, and they were coming toward us. We barely had time to get out the escape door. Garse, he saved us. And I saved your Bible. Here it is." And she reverently handed him the Bible.

They were all black with soot and smoke that had boiled down the cracks in the escape route. The children were frightened to the point of a trembling silence. Guard gathered them all into the circle of his arms crying, "Jesus loves us all."

Garse and Guard moved their families up to the church. There they found others of the community gathered. The men then set out to search the woods for others who may have escaped.

As they neared the church, the Indian boy refused to go inside. He pointed in and said, "God," and then he covered his ears. The picture was beginning to be clear. They had found him the morning after they had been told that the Indians were coming. This was on the first day of their revival meeting. The prayers and sounds of the lap organ had frightened the Indians. This also explained why the Indian was so scared when they prayed and sang. They didn't try to explain this to him, but decided to wait until he was more to be trusted.

This was just one of the times that they felt that God was watching over them. None of their people had been murdered. All had been accounted for. But these families had lost it all. They later learned that none of the outlying cabins had been burned. It was like a revenge, a final chapter to the previous raid. Garse had left his precious Bible and books in the church building where he had been studying. These, too, were unharmed. For some reason the Indians had left this building alone.

All of the root cellars and spring houses had enough food stored in them to see these families through the winter if they were careful. People came from all around with other supplies, and to help. Soon there were four new cabins standing in the community.

Once again, Guard placed wooden shutters on the open windows promising himself and his wife that he would go to the trading post and get glass panes and more muslin just as soon as he could.

Mr. Long made himself the self-appointed teacher of the Indian boy. He gave him the Christian name of Joseph, calling him Joe. Soon Mr. Long and Indian Joe were very close friends.

There was a great deal of concern for Katie after the Indian raid, but on March 11, 1776, she gave birth to a fine, healthy son. She named him Daniel Garse McCall. Daniel was chosen because he had already been through a fiery furnace and God had kept him through it.

They later learned that on the day that Daniel Garse McCall was born, the Indians had met with the representatives of the Henderson Land Company and other leaders at Sycamore Shoals, and had signed away many square miles of land to the white men.

Once again, the Cherokee War Chief had created a scene at this celebration by predicting trouble. And it happened, on

July 20, 1776, the Indians attacked Fort Watauga. They captured Mrs. William Bean, the wife of the white man who was already in the area when the Robertson party first arrived. She was unable to outrun them as she tried to make it to the fort. They had also captured a man named Thomas Moore. The Indians took them to their overhill town of refuge, Chota. There, they tortured Thomas Moore to death.

Mrs. Bean's life was spared by Nancy Ward, the same lovely Indian squaw who had amazed Matilda. The Indians tied her to a stake and had lit the fire. Nancy had run out and stomped the fire, shaming the braves for burning a squaw. The Indians kept her awhile to teach them how to make butter and cheese. Later, Nancy Ward, the Beloved Woman, smuggled her home.

The entire area was growing. Many settlers were coming in from North Carolina, and many from Virginia. Jonesborough was a town, and the center of activities for the entire area.

The settlements in the lower parts of the Nolichucky Valley at the foot of the Rich Mountains were growing. Many Presbyterians moved into the area, along with the Methodists and the Quakers. Other groups of Baptists also came in and organized. Religion was the most important thing, and the most driving factor in the lives of the members of all of these groups. This small group of Anabaptists called Freewillers also continued to grow. As news of their church carried across the mountains, they were joined by more people of like persuasion, until the little church could scarcely hold them all.

Chapter Fifteen

"Looks like war's a coming," Garse said to his brother one Sunday evening after church. "The brethren from the North Carolina Free Will Baptist group, who came over to visit with us, tell me that the talk of war is constant. They're meeting in Philadelphia now. I've always felt that it would come sooner or later. We'd better be thinking about it. Their freedom is also our freedom. You know, we're over here illegally—could be a lot of trouble."

Guard answered his brother slowly and thoughtfully, "I know. I heerd that Lt. Sevier is getting men mustered up. Guess he wants us to all be ready fer Red Coats or Red Skins, whichever. I heerd that they're musterin' up river at Red Banks at Greasy Cove. Guess we do need to get ready. Don't know what's gonna happen. Guess maybe that they're even musterin' in a little closer to us."

The preacher-brother answered, "We'll just have to ask the Lord's guidance for the church and for His people. He brought us here, He kept us here, and He will continue to keep us."

The next four years were ones of anxiety. There were numerous Indian attacks, but they were mostly in other areas. Yet the men kept drilling. The practice would be useful against both the Indians and the British. The colonies were now at war with England, but the battles as yet had not moved into the Southern Colonies. Tennessee would not become the sixteenth member of the Union until 1796, but they lived with the knowledge that any day they would be called upon to defend what was their heritage.

Garse and Katie had two more children, a girl and a boy. Guard's and Matilda's children were now six and eight years old, and another one would come in the spring.

Joseph, the Indian lad, had gone back to his people. He had learned the English language and had accepted Christ. His desire was to tell them that Jesus loved them. He couldn't join the braves in fighting or in hunting because he had healed from his injury with a very noticeable limp. Guard saw him occasionally when he went to one of the trading posts in the areas, and sometimes Joe would come back to the village to visit his Christian friends.

The fear of war in the mountains finally materialized. One morning Garse rode in rather quickly on his horse. "Guard," he called out, rather than to ride over to where Guard was with his family. Guard walked over to his brother. "Guard, we just got a message that the war for liberty against England has spread into the Carolinas. Reckon we're part and parcel of North Carolina, and there's several hundred men on this side of the Appalachian ridge. It just wouldn't be fair to let them fight our battles for us. 'Cause if they lose, we lose. If England wins, our freedom is gone. King George might even try to force us back into the Anglican Church."

Guard answered in his slow drawl, "Garse, you know I don't hold none to killin,' but I reckon we've got to protect what's ours. We'd better get our men together and go. We'll move your family into our bigger cabin, and leave Matilda's pa here to look after things."

"They're gatherin' over at Red Banks to go to Fort Watauga. They say we'll go back over the Roan Mountain Trail as soon's we can. We'd better get the word out." With this Garse rode off to another cabin to tell them.

The entire region of the Watauga Assembly covered a large section of land. So many men and boys volunteered to go fight the British that a draft was organized to choose those to remain in the Overmountain Settlements to protect the people and the property. Everyone worked. Women made and mended clothes. Millers ground corn for bread. Women baked it and prepared other foods. Others prepared bullets from powder at a small lead mine on the banks of the Nolichucky.

Then on Sept. 26, 1780, the women and children gathered in force at Sycamore Shoals at Fort Watauga to see their men off to war. Rev. Samuel Doak spoke to the men. He gave a short message on the need for freedom and the job they were called to do. Then he prayed. His touching prayer ended with, "Help us as good soldiers to wield the sword of the Lord and of Gideon." This became the marching theme and the battle cry for the ragged overmountain army! THE SWORD OF THE LORD AND OF GIDEON.

The trip was hard. The men had to walk for nearly two hundred miles over treacherous foot trails. Heavy rains hindered them. Somewhere along the way the Overmountain Army was informed that the British had a large supply of goods and ammunition for the Cherokees to use in attacking the settlements back on the Watauga and the Nolichucky Rivers. The British had formed an alliance with the Cherokees. They promised them all their land back if they would help fight the settlers in the mountain regions. The Cherokees arrived in Augusta, Georgia, to get these supplies and return to attack the settlers. On their way, they had been attacked by another army of ragged Americans, under Col. Clarke. The Indians had won. They had tortured and killed many of these men. A great number of the men had their families traveling with them. Many of them were also killed. The surviving people led by Col. Clarke ran for the mountains to hide. Many of them crossed over the ridge and through the gorges to safety with the Overmountain settlers.

This knowledge added to the distress in which these brothers found themselves. They spent a lot of time as they walked, praying and encouraging each other. They were so afraid that the Indians would follow the stragglers over the mountain and destroy their families. But this never materialized, because a bigger battle was forming.

This ragged army of settlers soon found themselves engaged in a battle that took their thoughts off of far away troubles. This battle pitted American against American. Men who wanted freedom fought against the Tories, who were Americans loyal to the king of England.

The mountain men, uniformless, ragged, and untrained in military finesse, soundly defeated British General Ferguson at Kings Mountain on Oct. 7, 1780. This was a major turning point in the war. After a few days of clean-up operations, they re-grouped to begin the march back over the mountains to home. The settlers turned soldiers left some buried at Kings Mountain, and some were being carried back wounded.

Among the wounded was Guard. A musket ball had hit his leg, shattering a bone. The wound was so severe that he could not travel. Garse and others from Sevier's troops made a travois to pull him to an area of wooded land where they felt he would be safe from the Tory sympathizers. Guard was delirious. His fever was raging, and he spoke out of his head. In his delirium he spoke to Daniel Boone. He begged Mr. Forrester not to beat him. He talked to his children and sang hymns with Matilda. Sometimes he talked with God.

"It's no use, Garse," the camp doctor said as he shook his head sadly. "The leg is gone. We'll have to amputate."

Garse's face was ashen white, "When, Doctor?"

"As soon as we can do it. Let's get a fire going. We'll need plenty of boiling water," the doctor answered.

"Doctor," asked Garse with a whispered plea, "can it wait until tomorrow morning? Can you just wait and see what happens?"

"Yes and no," the doctor said. "I can, but I don't recommend it. Every minute we wait is working against him. Infection has already set in. But we'll try. We'll wait as long as possible."

The preacher-man from the lower settlements of the Nolichucky River in the Watauga Assembly gathered the men around him whom he knew from the settlements. All he asked them was, "Can you pray?" Some were from other Baptist groups, some from Doak's churches, the Presbyterians, and others from his own little church called Liberty Hill. They all quoted Scriptures that they remembered, Scriptures that were promises from God's Word. Garse led in a little talk on "If ye ask in faith believing that will I do." The group prayer lasted for a good half hour, then they divided into shifts and kept a prayer vigil all night.

Even a group of scoffers and hard-core sinners took on an atmosphere of reverence and respect. Tears flowed down many cheeks of these calloused men. They settled down into a respectful quiet the rest of the night.

Several times during the night the doctor checked on Guard. There didn't seem to be any difference in his condition. Then, just as the sun broke over the eastern horizon, Guard began to sing, "I'm marching to Zion, beautiful, beautiful Zion. I'm marching upward to Zion, the beautiful city of God."

This frightened many of them. They thought that they were witnessing a death-bed scene. But not Garse. He began to rejoice, "Glory, Glory, the Hand of the Lord has spared him," he cried. Then Garse and the others knelt to pray a prayer of thanksgiving.

The doctor was amazed. The fever was down, and the infection was much less than it had been the night before. He asknowledged that it was a miracle.

Just a few days after the men had left for Kings Mountain, a group of weary, nearly starved people came across the most rugged of mountain passes from North Carolina over the Appalachian Ridge. They told a horrible story of Indian and British intrigue planned against the Overmountain settlers. These people had to run for their lives. Some of their family members had been captured by the Cherokees. Many were tortured and killed. People all over the mountain valleys took these refugees into their homes.

All work had stopped except necessary farm chores and cooking. The people were living and moving but not with any show of energy. Each day Matilda, Katie, and the others vainly watched for some sign of a messenger with news of the battle, or better yet, to see their men folks returning. They also lived in a state of suspenseful worry, waiting and watching for an Indian attack.

Matilda's pa gathered them together. "How big is our God?" he asked. "Does not His arm stretch to North Carolina? He has protected us before and will continue to protect us here and protect our loved ones there. Let us pray about this."

Gradually the men began to arrive home. Most had mustered out at Sycamore Shoals. They brought word about the battle and the victory. They brought news of Guard's injury and about his miraculous recovery from the jaws of death.

They told that Garse and three other men would be along later. Guard was being brought in on a pallet. They had sent them word to pray for good weather and safety from Indians as they traveled.

During the time of their waiting for them to return home, Matilda's mother died. Although the grief was almost unbearable, they were comforted by her testimony in Jesus Christ. Since her immersion and her membership in their little church, she had grown in grace and in the Lord. She wasn't an old woman, yet years of hard wilderness living had exacted a heavy toll from her.

Matilda yearned more and more for the comforts of her husband. She tried to keep busy so she wouldn't worry to the point of frustration. Joshua was almost nine and Mary Kate seven. She and Katie spent long hours teaching them in their books. The days were getting shorter and cooler. She and her pa tried hard to keep all of the chores done up. Older men from the church came by often to help with the tedious and difficult chores.

But, still no McCall brothers.

One unusually cold evening in early November, the wind and rain beat strongly against the cabin. They had finished the chores as quickly as possible and settled down by the fireside. Pa got the Bible and began reading, "If ye ask anything in my name...."

Matilda looked up, "Pa, let's do it. Let's pray. This weather is bad. Guard needs protection from it. He'll take the fever and die. Let's pray, Pa. Let's pray in His name."

The family knelt to pray, even the children. They prayed for a long time. Pa had told them that they would pray until they got hold of the horns of the altar, and after awhile, Pa said, "Amen."

Nine-year-old Joshua spoke up with a broken voice, "Forever and ever, Amen."

Pa banked the fire and they went to bed. Soon all were sleeping. Matilda went to sleep with more peace of mind than she had any night since the men had left to go to war. She felt reassured of the Lord that all was well.

Later in the night she was awakened rather suddenly. She

sat up, "Was that the wind blowing? Pa, Pa, wake up, come here."

Together, she and Pa went to the door. The wind was so fierce they could hardly be heard speaking to each other. "Who is it?" Pa asked.

A hoarse, weak voice was heard through the storm's violence, "We're home."

By this time Kate and her family had climbed down out of the loft where they were staying. Joshua and Mary Kate were awake and standing in the middle of the floor. Then, Garse and Indian Joe were standing wet and cold inside the little room. They were holding up a cold and wet, but happy Guard. Everyone was laughing and crying and talking at one time.

Guard raised his hand. "I think that we need to stop and thank God for deliverance." He bowed his head. "Dear Lord, we are thankful for a great God that leads His children every step through this weary land. In Jesus' name."

They stood there quietly and Guard finished the prayer, "Forever and ever, Amen."

Pa walked over to put a log on the fire. Guard looked around as if looking for something or someone. "Where is Ma?" he whispered.

Matilda looked up. Tears were overflowing. She shook her head and said, "Gone." Then she was in his arms sobbing, yielding forth all the tears that had been stored up for all these weeks. She was no longer brave, nor did she feel a need for bravery. Her man was home.

Guard comforted her the best he could and let her cry. He knew that crying was the best medicine to express sorrow for her mother, and also to show her joy for his return.

After awhile Guard spoke, "Let us tell you about Indian Joe. He was down at the Old Towns, near the Tenasi River, when some of the Cherokee warriors returned from the battle with Col. Clarke at Augusta. He heard from them about the battle at Kings Mountain, and about all us mountainmen walkin' down there. He wanted to find out effen any of us went. So, he traveled around to the tradin' posts nearby. A'fore long he heerd a story 'bout one of the Overmountain men having a leg wound and the men prayin' fer him, and his leg being spared. I'll give ye the details later. Joe figgered it was one of us...cause of our faith in prayer. So he came lookin' fer us. Effen it hadn't been for Indian Joe, well, I don't even want to think about what might a happened." With that, he hugged Joe like a brother.

The entire community was awakened the next morning by the ringing of the church bell. It rang for quite a spell. It wasn't long until the little church was filled with settlers. This prayer meeting was the forerunner of a great revival in the settlement.

Chapter Sixteen

After the War for Independence, more and more and more white settlers moved into the area, and many of the refugees from Clarke's army who had escaped the Indians decided to stay in the Overmountain settlements.

Many settlers who lived by unwritten rules of war figured that the spoils belonged to the victors. Since the Indians and the British were fighting as allies and were defeated, then the Indians had no more right to the land. Many white settlers dishonestly took advantage of the Indians. Some of them continued the war by tracking the Indians on to their towns and waging war and defeating them. This marked the beginning of the end of Cherokee strength. The Chickamauga Indians were also defeated at the Battle of Lookout Mountain. After this there was only an occasional incident with the Indians.

It was only a short while after this that a group of settlers went down stream to French Salt Lick in the Cumberland area. They were led by James Robertson. This migration led to the establishment of the city of Nashville. Indian troubles would follow them, for this area was still Indian territory.

All of the Overmountain lands were officially called Washington County, North Carolina. In 1783, the North Carolina Assembly divided Washington County and created Greene County. The land that they called Greene County covered much of what is now Tennessee.

On August 23, 1784, many Overmountain farmers met in Jonesborough in a first step to form a new state. Their leader once again was John Sevier, known to them as Nolichucky Jack. And once again, this led to the taking of sides. Those who wanted to be part of this new state, to be called Franklin, were loyal to Sevier. But there were those who were loyal to the North Carolina government. This move for statehood, which was favored by President Jefferson, almost succeeded. It failed within four years, but not without bloodshed. Unscrupulous leaders in North Carolina again aroused the Indian hopes of restored lands and persuaded them to once again join in battle against the Overmountain men.

So this time, 1789, it wasn't Guard, nor Garse, called into battle, but seventeen-year-old Joshua. There had already been small battles all over the Watauga Assembly. Hatred was seen and felt in the affairs of the people. There had been several men killed, among them the brother of John Sevier. And now, Lt. Sevier was calling for men to fight with him against those in North Carolina and their Indian allies, who opposed the state of Franklin.

Guard and Matilda were proud of Joshua, but both of them felt as if their hearts would break. Wilderness living and freedom had been so costly. Guard's crippling walk and his inability to do a lot of his farm chores were a constant reminder of this. Guard, himself, was only thrity-six, but the ravages of wilderness life and war had aged him immensely. He had a dread that his son could end up just like he was. Even Matilda, at age 34, was still lovely, though tired looking. The last seventeen years had given her five babies, with the last two not surviving infancy.

Their daughter, born after the Battle of Kings Mountain, had deep auburn hair like her pa, and they had named her Molly, after Matilda's mother. And then there was their older daughter, Mary Kate. She had married a young son of the Coggin's family, who had become a Free Will Baptist preacher and had moved to the Stoney Creek section of the Watauga settlement.

But to have their only son go off to battle with the Indians was a hard thing. Indians could be so tricky. Any war was bad, but this one concerned them terribly. It was so close by, just over the Rich Mountains, where the Nolichucky River meandered as it flowed toward them. This area was called Flint Creek and was high in the mountains south of the same Red Banks where Guard had mustered under Lt. Sevier for Kings Mountain.

As they watched their son and the sons of the other settlers ride down the road toward their mustering-in place, they thought that their hearts would break, but there was nothing that they could do about it, nothing, that is, but pray.

The battle lasted only about one-half hour. That is one-half hour after Lt. Sevier's men began to fight Indian style. When the battle was over, the settlers had lost five men, and the Indians had lost one hundred and forty-five men. They were thankful and grateful that Joshua was not injured. This was to be the last major battle with Indians in the Overmountain lands.

So they settled down to the business of living. It was still a very hard life. Indians had not been the only factor that had brought a struggle to these pioneers. They had to fight against the elements and against illness, but gradually they built up their strength in number and in property.

The McCalls built onto their farm until it contained almost all they needed to be self-sufficient. What they did not have the community had: a blacksmith shop, a mill, and a place for making vinegar and candles. They could tan leather and even make their own shoes now. Everyone there worked and cooperated together. This in itself made life easier.

The church had grown. They had a pump organ now, but the older folks still enjoyed telling about Mrs. Coggins' lap organ and the Indians. The children never tired of hearing about it. The church hired a music man to come and hold a singing school. With what he taught them, it wasn't long until Molly was playing the organ.

Guard, himself, enjoyed the singing school as much as the young people, and not to be outdone by them, he soon mastered the shape notes; Me 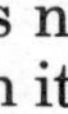 , faw 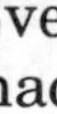 , sol 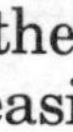 , and law  . He would often slip over to the church and take a seat at the organ. Pumping it was very difficult because of his crippled leg, but he enjoyed trying. He used his private moments at the organ as another means of worshiping God. He would lustily and loudly play and sing, "I Am Bound For The Promised Land."

Indian Joe had moved nearby. He wanted to learn more about God, and he needed the Christian fellowship. He didn't stay there all of the time, for he visited the Indians towns often to tell them more about the Jesus who loved them.

More than once, Guard was heard to express his sincere and heartfelt feelings that God was better to them than to anyone he knew.

After being under territorial government for awhile, North Carolina gave up their claim to the area. All this land which was called the Territory Southwest of the River Ohio became the sixteenth state, Tennessee, on June 1, 1796. John Sevier was the first governor. And farther down the state, the same James Robertson who led the ragged group across the Roan Mountain, and the other group down river to French Salt Lick, was a leader in its development.

No longer was the entire area of the Nolichucky River Valley a wilderness. Towns were growing. Andrew Johnson had opened a tailor shop in Greeneville and had gone on into politics. Andy Jackson had a law office in Jonesborough. A family named Crockett lived on the other side of the river not far from the Liberty Hill community. Serveral businesses were opening. Stagecoach roads were cut from town to town. Liberty Hill community on the banks of the Nolichucky River in the Overmountain country was not so far removed from the rest of the world.

Education was a major factor in their growth. Samuel Doak had organized two schools in the area that had been Jacob Brown's claim. One called Doak's Log College was farther up the river closer to Jonesborough. It was later to be called Washington College Academy. The other was very close to their settlement and was called Tusculum. Both of these were chartered by the Presbyterian Church.

Joshua had chosen to attend Tusculum College. Before leaving he said, "Pa, I don't want you to worry none about me. I'm firm in what I believe. I want to learn, Pa. I want to be able to come back here and help our people, Pa. And Pa, the Lord wants me to preach. I can learn there. There's men of God there—men who can pray. You said yourself that Samuel Doak had power with God. And Pa, I'll be home every chance I get. I've got a good horse, and I can work hard, so I'll make it. Will you help me, Pa? Mostly, will you pray for me?"

Tears filled Guard's eyes. Tears of joy. His son would be able to read and study and learn. And he would preach. This was an answer to all his prayers, prayers that he had prayed ever since he, himself, had accepted the Lord way back in Garse's cabin on Willow Branch, in North Carolina. So, he answered, "Certainly, Son, ye've got my blessin.' God bless ye. I always wanted ye to be a preacher-boy. I prayed for that end." He wiped away the tears as they mingled with his smile.

Epilogue

The winter of 1844,45 was a very cold one in the Nolichucky Valley. Guard's bad leg ached, sometimes almost unbearably. Many nights he sat by the open fire all night baking it and reading from his Book and praying. He was an old man now. He was ninety-two years old, and had outlived his brother, Garse; Garse's wife, Katie; and his own beloved Matilda. Even his preacher-boy son, Joshua, had been gone three years now. But Joshua's son, his namesake, Guard, was also a preacher-boy and was pastoring the Liberty Hill Free Will Baptist Church. Molly, his youngest, was getting along in years. The entire valley was filled with descendants of the older pioneers and with memories of their struggles and victories. Guard often remarked to his family and friends that he had more on Heaven's shore than on this side. He closed each prayer with a request that he might soon go Home.

Spring came, warm winds blew. The mountains broke out in full dress of spring blossoms. Guard picked up his cane and carrying his Bible in the other hand, climbed up the hill to his resting place under one of his apple trees. He looked around him. Things had changed in the seventy-four years he had been here. Most of these changes had been for the better.

He looked at his beloved church. A church that had sometimes stood alone in what they believed to be the truth of God's Word. A church that believed in living separated lives and tried to hold to the Word as they saw it. It had just recently become part of the Toe River Association of Free Will Baptists in Western North Carolina. The building was no longer a log structure, but was now covered with white wood siding.

He looked at the orchard around him, bordered by the grape arbor. Grapes planted just to have juice for their communion services. This had always been Matilda's job, and now Molly took care of it.

He looked at the creek which cut deep trenches into the soft limestone. He thought of all the folks who had been baptized there: Matilda's parents, Matilda, Indian Joe, all their children, their friends, and even himself.

Then, his gaze swept up to the graveyard, on a hill the other side of the church, to Indian Joe's grave. He had come home in time to die, just to have a Christian burial. Guard wiped away a tear.

And there in the graveyard were the McCall graves. The little ones, the babies that he never got to see grow up. He felt consoled knowing that they were now with their mother, his beloved Matilda. And there were big graves too, all of those that he had outlived.

He looked down at his Book and he opened it and read, "The Spirit and the Bride say, Come, And let him that heareth say, Come, And let him that is athirst come...."

Guard heard a voice, "Grandpa, Grandpa." He looked down the hill toward the cabin. Molly's golden haired granddaughter, little Matilda, was calling to him.

Before he could answer her, he heard another voice and he looked up. "Guard," this voice called, "come up hither."

And Guard McCall called back, "I'm coming, Lord."